I0525173

BRAIN GAMES

ALEX P. BERG

BATDOG PRESS

KNOXVILLE, TN

Copyright © 2016 by Alex P. Berg

All rights reserved. No part of this publication may be reproduced, distributed or transmitted in any form or by any means, including photocopying, recording, or other electronic or mechanical methods, without the prior written permission of the publisher, except in the case of brief quotations embodied in critical reviews and certain other non-commercial uses permitted by copyright law. For permission requests, contact the publisher:

Batdog Press
www.batdogpress.com

Publisher's Note: This is a work of fiction. Names, characters, places, and incidents portrayed in this novel are a product of the author's imagination.

Cover Art: Damon Za
Book Layout: ©2013 BookDesignTemplates.com

Brain Games / Alex P. Berg — 1st ed.
ISBN 978-1-942274-21-6

1

The hot rays of Tau Ceti filtered down through the sky, cutting through distant cirrus fragments as they barreled pell-mell toward the gleaming hulls of freighters, cutters, and clippers, Kestrels™ and Photons™, which stretched for kilometers along the wide expanse of the sales lot. The air rippled with latent heat, the pavement hissed and moaned, and I thanked science for the shade drone that hovered overhead, misting me with chilled rose water.

A short, stocky man stood next to me in the shade patch, impeccably dressed in an ivory-colored Hempette jacket and matching dress shorts. His heavily-styled bouffant hair glistened unnaturally from the drone's mist, but better that than faint under the sun's barrage.

He cast his hand toward a sleek, glossy ship in front of us and launched into another spiel. "Now this is a craft I think might be right up your alley, Mr. Weed. The Kestrel™ Chinook Z-Class, part of their Zephyr line. A sleek one hundred thousand kilograms, capable of a continuous fusion-powered, resonant cavity-driven thrust of over five million Newtons—a ludicrously high amount for a ship of this weight, so don't say I didn't warn you. Just be sure to invest in a top of the line pressure suit before you get frisky with the throttle. But in case you were thinking this was merely a racer, think again. The Chinook features quarters for four, each impeccably equipped with multi-purpose retractable furnishings and appliances. Separate washrooms. And don't even get me started on the cockpit..."

Stan, as he'd introduced himself upon my arrival at the shipyard, gestured aggressively with his hands as he talked, alternating between finger guns jabbed toward the ships in question or held vertically as a frame to his face. His style grated on me. Personally, I would've much preferred a sales droid over the man's irritating delivery, but androids, as calm and cool as they were, couldn't provide that 'human touch' so desired in high priced spaceship sales. Besides, droids were terrible negotiators due to their programmed predispositions of kindness, subservience, and respect toward humans.

I wiped a bit of chilled mist from my brow with the back of my hand, checking on the resilience of my own pomade-styled hair as I did so. Stan droned on about friction regulators, gold-plated toilet seats, and any number of other equally useless add-ons that would only serve to inflate my ego and the purchase price of the vehicle in question.

I waved a hand at Stan. "Yes, yes. I think I can live without that particular piece of junk. What I want to know is...does it have an Alcubierre drive?"

Before he could answer, a derisive sniff drew my attention to the side.

I turned to stare at Carl, my android manservant and onetime nursemaid turned sleuthing partner. He stood next to Stan's hovercart outside the edge of the drone's shadow, not a single droplet of sweat rolling through his short shorn blond hair despite the Cetie heat and the dark green tartan jacket draping his shoulders—one of the perks of his inorganic origins. A smirk curled one corner of his lips, but it didn't do anything to mar his otherwise perfectly chiseled features.

I cleared my throat. "You, ah...have something to add?"

Carl met my eyes. "Passive-aggressive behavior doesn't suit you. You know exactly why I sniffed. We discussed it before. Warp drive technology is tremendously energy intensive. A reactor potent enough to power an Alcubierre drive is probably going to weigh in excess of fifty thousand kilograms alone, never mind the drive itself or the resonant cavity thrusters you'd still need for intrastellar and terrestrial transport. You're not going to find that technology on a ship of this size."

"You don't know that for a fact," I said. "Perhaps there have been technological advancements in warp drive function since the last time we checked."

Carl rolled his eyes, which was a plain enough answer for me.

I turned back to Stan. "Carl's right, I assume?"

Stan nodded. "Unfortunately yes, sir. Warp drives simply aren't an option on ships within this weight class. But the Chinook is a superb vehicle in every other regard. Fast. Sleek. Comparatively affordable. Perhaps I could give you a tour of the inside?"

Comparatively was the operative term. I'd received a massive windfall from my last case with interstellar transport titan InterSTELLA, but even their largesse only stretched so far. "I'm not sure an intrastellar vehicle is going to cut it. I want more freedom than that. Isn't there anything with an Alcubierre drive within my price range?"

"Remind me again, sir," said Stan. "That was...?"

"About six millions SEUs," I said. "Although I could probably push it to...*nine?*"

Carl winced at my negotiating skills, and given his predispositions, that said something.

Stan scrunched his face. "Ah. Yes. Well...it's *possible*. I don't think we have anything in our catalog that could be purchased at that price *new*, but if we expand our search to pre-owned vessels we might be able to find a contender. Perhaps a used corvette or a even a freighter, if it's a bit of a jalopy—er, I mean, fixer-upper. Let me run a search through our servenets..."

Stan trailed off with that glazed look indicative of active Brain usage—Brains, of course, being the organically-integrated computing systems the vast majority of us had implanted into our cerebral cortexes shortly after birth. While some chose to forgo them—or more accurately, some parents chose for their children to forgo them—those of us who weren't science-hating hippies benefitted greatly. Brains provided us instant access to the public servenets, putting the collective knowledge of the sentient races at the tips of our nerve endings. We could take part in immersive Brain experiences that simulated sights, sounds, smells, tastes, and physical sensations, even in the most private and sensual of ways, and we could watch vids of cats falling into bathtubs at a moment's notice.

Want me to queue one up?

Without waiting for an answer, my own Brain's curator, Paige, overlaid a montage vid of feline fails into the corner of my vision.

I suppressed a chuckle as an unfortunate tabby backflipped into a bucket and mentally waved Paige off. *Not now. I've got business.*

She obliged me by turning the vid off, but not before shooting off her mouth. *You started it with your unhealthy obsession of watching animals injure themselves.*

'Unhealthy' seemed a touch much, but I'd long since learned to take Paige's barbs with a grain of salt. Ultimately, her verbal sparring was more my fault than hers. When initializing her so many moons past, I'd chosen bubbly and cynical as her primary personality parameters, and she'd only grown more gleefully combative as the years rolled by, all in response to my own behavior. She was clever like that. While she might've not *technically* been conscious, she was as close as you could come without crossing the line.

Stan surfaced from his delve into the digital deep, his eyes clearing. "Yes, as I suspected. We don't have anything in stock to fit your needs, here or in our other locations on Cetie. But I've put in a query to our sister locations on Cetif. It's possible we'll find something within your price range."

Carl cleared his throat. "Rich, could I speak with you? Privately?"

"Excuse me for a moment," I said to Stan.

The man smiled and nodded, but I imagined he secretly wilted inside, both at the prospect of losing the healthy commission he stood to gain from my ship purchase and from losing the drone's cover and cool mist.

I walked a few dozen paces with Carl, the drone shadowing me—literally—before stopping just beyond the Chinook's portside wing. "Yes, Carl? What is it?"

My longtime friend glanced at Stan before training his cool blue eyes on me. "Rich...why are we here?"

"Please tell me there's some hidden metaphysical meaning to that question I'm not grasping, because if you can't figure out what we're doing in a shipyard being shown vessels by a spaceship salesman, then I'm going to have to take you in for maintenance."

"Can't sneak anything by you," said Carl. "What I meant is, what's with the sudden fascination with buying your own vessel?"

"We talked about this," I said. "Something about our last case with InterSTELLA got my explorative juices flowing—something you and your fluid-free interior can't quite seem to grasp. It would be fun to explore the galaxy between investigations, and beyond that, so long as I take a few cases off planet, I can write the purchase off as a business expense."

"You're right," said Carl. "I don't understand this burning desire to liberate yourself of the ten million SEU bounty you just earned, but if for some reason you're dead set on purchasing your own spacecraft rather than buying tickets on an InterSTELLA transport like any normal person would, could you at least reconsider this warp drive fascination? Dropping five to six million SEUs on a top of the line Kestrel™ is one thing, but bankrupting yourself to purchase a beat up old freighter is insane."

"What's the point of owning a craft without an Alcubierre drive, though?" I said. "There's only so much to see in the Tau Ceti system. What am I supposed to do? Take laps from here to the gloomy, cloud-ridden skies of Cetif, over to the space casino circling Cetib, and back? Where's the fun in that?"

"You know you can buy tickets for your ship on larger freighters, right? You park your vessel in the hold, let the freighter worry about the warp burn, and once you arrive in a new star system, you fly back out. All the freedom of having your own Alcubierre drive with none of the hassle. Or the cost."

I furrowed my brows. "I don't know. You're still dependant on others. It's not *complete* freedom. But your point about cost isn't lost on me, and I do hate renovations."

A trill sounded in the back of my head, that of a Brain call. I waited for Paige to fill me in.

It's to your work line, Paige said after a moment. *Originating from a Helena Busk. Care to take it?*

My recent financial windfall had made it so I didn't need to take any cases, but money was only one of many reasons I'd decided to enter the private investigation field. I'd been independently wealthy before I'd ever set foot in my office, after all—the lucky recipient of my grandfather's extensive land lease from his recreational marijuana plantation.

"Sure," I said. "Patch her in."

A voice sprung to life in the back of my head, but only a voice. No corresponding visual feed came through, which was a little odd, but some people preferred it that way.

Hello? Mr. Weed?

Yes. Rich Weed, private investigator, at your service Miss...Busk, I believe?

That's correct. Pleased to meet you. Her voice, or the Brain representation thereof, came across as strong, smooth, and confident.

Likewise, I said. *How can I help you?*

Well, Mr. Weed, she said. *I was hoping I could engage your services. There's an individual I'm looking to track down, and your name was the first I chanced across in the biz listings under private investigators.*

Helena was being generous. Likely my name was the *only* one in the biz listings under that designation. It was the last time I checked.

Certainly, Miss Busk, I said. *I'd love to help you with that, but at the moment I'm in the middle of a business transaction. Could you pop by my office to discuss this in greater detail in, say...forty-five minutes?*

Silence stretched for several seconds, and I thought for a moment Paige had lost the call. Eventually, Helena responded, but her voice had turned hesitant and hitching. *You...want me to...come by your office?*

Is that a problem?

More silence. Longer than the first. *Ah...no. No problem. It'll be a good exercise for me. I think...*

Sometimes I'm not the quickest on the draw—I blamed my years as a professional kickboxer for my occasional mental lapses—but even I picked up on the problem. Helena's sudden transformation from a calm, confident woman to a skittish mouse coincided suspiciously with my request to meet her face to face, hinting at a certain pervasive personality type.

We called them Intros. Unlike Extros, who relished in personal contact, Intros preferred to spend their hours immersed in Brain games and experiences over real world interactions. Their emergence had tracked closely with advancements in virtual reality, but their numbers exploded once Brain technology hit its stride in the early thirty-two hundreds. It was one thing to be able to see, hear, and smell events in a virtual world, but with Brain technology, virtual spaces became fully immersive, offering sensations of taste, balance, movement, and touch, and in every extremity of the body no less—including the naughty bits. Some people became so addicted they never left the house, and thanks to guaranteed basic incomes provided by governments due to the prevalence of droid labor, they didn't have to.

I proceeded with a bit of newfound compassion, but not an excessive amount. My mother had been an Intro, and I still resented her lack of involvement in my life. *Well, if you like, we could meet virtually—though I prefer to greet my clients face to face.*

No, no, it's alright, said Helena. *As I said, this will be a good exercise for me.*

I kept a snide remark about Intros and exercise to myself. *Very well. I'll send you the address. Forty-five minutes, then?*

I couldn't hear the sigh, but I envisioned it. *Yes. I'll do my best.*

The Brain call cut out. Carl stared at me with a raised brow, but not because he didn't know what had transpired. Paige copied him on all my Brain transmissions except for the personal ones.

Oh, I copy him on those, too, snickered Paige.

Fine. The excessively personal ones, then.

"So," said Carl. "Three-quarters of an hour, is it? Given our distance from the office, that means we'll have to head out shortly."

I shot him an affected smile. "I know, and *yes,* that means I've decided to think the ship purchase over. Don't let it go to your head. We might come back here before everything is said and done."

Carl tried to hide his own smile, but failed. "Very well. Let's go break the bad news to Stan before he melts."

2

I rapped my fingers against my cherry wood desk and stared at the door. The etched lettering in the frosted glass, inverted horizontally from my point of view, read 'RICH WEED, PREMIUM INVESTIGATIVE SERVICES.'

It refused to open.

"Maybe she got lost," said Carl.

He sat in one of the plush chairs facing my desk, his right leg crossed over his left and his tartan-draped arms spread out wide upon the armrests. Midafternoon sunlight showered through the floor-to-ceiling windows at my back, sending shadows dripping from my couch and club chair quartet into the lab-grown fox fur rug that covered the right-hand side of my office. Up against the left-hand wall, a vintage polished copper espresso machine gurgled and sputtered as it brewed me a fresh cup of java—my second.

"Paige...the hour?" I asked.

Twenty-two forty, standard galactic time, she said. *Which means its been just shy of two hours since your conversation with Miss Busk.*

"She could've gotten stuck in traffic," said Carl.

"Paige?" I asked. "Traffic report?"

Nothing out of the ordinary. No major street congestion, and the tubes are running on time. Her Brain listing didn't include an address, but by my calculations, she could be living as far as fifteen hundred kilometers away and still be here by now, assuming she got a tube ticket on short notice.

I glanced at Carl. "You knew that already, didn't you?"

He shrugged. "No comment."

The coffee maker spat a few times and stilled. I stood and crossed over to get the cup. "Maybe it's time we admit she's not showing. I should've known better. Trying to coerce an Intro into a face-to-face meeting..." I shook my head.

"Coerce is a strong word," said Carl. "You merely asked. She acquiesced. And if you're that concerned over her absence, you can always call her back."

I waved him off as I sat back down with my coffee, its rich scent filling my nostrils. "Don't be silly. I'm not that desperate—for clients, cases, or cash. I just hope this poor woman didn't suffer a heart attack upon leaving her apartment. If she's a severe Intro, the shock of being in public could've done her in, especially if she took the tube."

If she were that introverted, she never would've agreed to meet you in the first place, offered Paige.

I nodded in agreement, but before I could further the conversation, a chime sounded. I shifted my eyes to the front door and noticed a shadow on the other side.

I perked up. "Come in."

The door winked open upon my command. In its wake stood a woman of average Cetie height, about a meter sixty, with light brown shoulder length hair, soft features, and relatively little muscle tone. Pervasive genetic engineering that selected for effortless muscle growth along with our planet's high gravitational pull made it difficult for Cetieans to avoid building lean muscle mass, but difficult was not the same as impossible as evidenced by the physiques of many Intro gamers. The woman wore a light gray tent dress that left her arms bare while hiding her waistline. A wide-brimmed hat and a pair of oversized sunglasses concealed much of her face.

I stood. "Miss Busk?"

She hesitated, like a wild animal caught in a beam of light.

I kept my movements to a minimum. "Don't worry. I won't bite. Take your time."

I couldn't see through her glasses, but her head tilted ever so slightly in my direction. Her breast rose and fell with several large breaths. After a moment, she moved her lips, but no words came out—or at least none that were audible to human ears.

"Pardon?" I said.

Helena tried again, a little louder. "I said, perhaps if you sat down that would help."

I blinked as I processed her request. Did she also think in terms of animal metaphors, making me the wolf to her rabbit? Did my bulk and height—a whopping ten centimeters greater than hers—intimidate her so?

Just sit down, you lummox, said Paige.

I did as I was told, but not before thinking I might regret leaving the spaceship lot for this case after all.

Helena inched her way closer one step at a time. As she neared the empty chair in front of my desk, she reached out and latched onto it, pulling herself into its embrace. Her breast continued to rise and fall, perhaps even faster than before, but certainly not from exertion. She kept her eyes averted to the side, refusing to meet my gaze.

I gave her a moment as I sipped my coffee. When I felt it was safe, I ventured forth. "So, Miss Busk. If I may—"

She shot back up, lip quivering and shaking her head. "No. Sorry. Can't do it. I can't do it. It's too much. I'm not ready. Maybe someday, but—"

"Miss Busk, if I may," said Carl in a soothing voice. "Would it help if you spoke to me instead? I'm Carl, Mr. Weed's personal droid. You can avert your eyes from him if it makes it easier."

Helena paused, one foot already pointed at the door as she considered Carl's plea. It shouldn't have made any difference her talking to Carl instead of me, but psychology was a fickle mistress. Despite the fact that Carl looked indistinguishable from a human—albeit not one of Cetiean descent, given his lighter build—simply knowing he wasn't a real person could make all the difference.

She nodded and sank back into her chair, making sure not to turn her head toward me. She took a deep breath and sighed. "Very well. I think I can do that, Mr...."

"Weatherby," said Carl, shifting his arms and shoulders toward Helena to appear more inviting. "Carlton Weatherby. But please, call me Carl. Everyone else does. Can I get you a beverage before we begin?"

Helena shook her head.

"So what brings you here?"

"Well, as I mentioned over the Brain call, I'm in search of someone. A relative. My...son, actually."

Helena paused and dipped her head, perhaps in contemplation. Carl wisely remained silent. I followed suit, though I might've slurped as I sipped my coffee.

"We've...become estranged, you see," she said. "I haven't spoken to him in thirty years. I haven't seen him in almost forty. And if I'm being honest, I never had any desire to during that time. I know how awful that sounds, but it's true. Which isn't to say I don't regret it. In my defense, I lost contact with a number of friends and family. I couldn't stand to see any of them, you understand. I lost myself in gaming, as I suspect my son has."

"Don't punish yourself over it," said Carl. "It's a more common occurrence than you might think."

That was an understatement. I'd suffered through much the same relationship with my own mother, a severe Intro and heavy gamer who decided to have me in a late-middle age hysteria and virtually never spoke to me after the fact. Unfortunately, I'd never had a chance to reconcile with her before her passing. Even after her death, I felt indifference toward her, but I'm sure our failed relationship was responsible for some quirk of mine.

You want a list to choose from? said Paige.

Be glad Carl reared me, I told her. *Imagine the psyche you'd have to deal with without his nurturing influence.*

I'd rather not.

Carl continued. "So this son of yours. His name is...?"

"Lars Busk," said Helena. "He's about sixty-five years of age."

Carl didn't ask her own age—not that it mattered. Thanks to extensive genetic engineering, most people stayed fresh-faced and healthy until their mid two-hundreds.

"To your knowledge, is Lars living on Cetie?" asked Carl.

Helena nodded. "I believe so. He's in the public listings."

"He is?" Carl lifted an eyebrow. "And you've reached out via Brain?"

Helena nodded again. "Yes, but he won't answer my calls. I fear he doesn't have any interest in reconnecting—which I understand given the circumstances, but I... I wanted to tell him. In person..."

Carl gave her a moment. "Tell him what?"

Helena took a slow breath. "His father and I separated many years ago, in part because of my gaming addiction. Maybe Lars resented me for it, or maybe he sought the same addiction I did for solace. Either way, I received word a couple days ago. His father passed. A freak accident during a spacecraft landing. I guess it made me...reconsider the value of my relationships."

Carl was slow to answer. "My condolences. Trust me, we'll do our best to find Lars, and assuming we do, I'm sure we'll be able to help. Act as intermediaries of sorts. If nothing else, we should be able to deliver a message."

Helena dipped her head again. A wet streak trickled down onto her cheek from underneath her sunglasses. "Please do. I'd appreciate your efforts."

"Of course," said Carl. "Now, there's the matter of our business arrangement. We have a standard contract—"

Helena stood, wiping away the tear as she did so. "I'm sorry to cut you short, but I've had about as much as I can handle of...*this*. You. And...him." She waved at me nervously. "I told myself I should give it a shot, as I'm going to have to interact with Lars should you find him, but I'm about at my wits' end. I'm sorry. Send me the contract via Brain. I'll look it over and return it. Goodbye...and thank you."

Helena whisked off toward the door, which closed behind her with a puff.

"Well, good thing I have you here," I said as I lifted my cup to my lips. "Otherwise, who'd run interference between me and the weirdoes?"

Carl gave me a nose downturned look. "You're in the service industry. Ever heard the motto, 'The customer is always right?'"

I took another sip of espresso and set my cup down. "You're correct, as always. I'm simply letting unwelcome familial memories crop up. They're clouding my judgment. Other than not being able to make eye contact, Helena seemed quite pleasant."

"So you're willing to take on her case?"

I nodded. "Why not? Sounds easy enough. It'll serve as a distraction while I mull those spacecraft options over."

"So I imagine the first step is to reach out to Lars via Brain?" asked Carl.

"The *first* step is to send Helena a contract," I said. "As much as I enjoy the mental aspects of private investigation, I can't set a bad precedent of working pro bono. But you're spot on with the second step to take. Hopefully Lars will be more receptive of our advances than those of his mother."

3

Our car slowed to a halt, and I leaned over to look out the window. We'd stopped in front of a ten story hunk of concrete that looked as if it had been extruded through a die. Rows of tinted windows dotted the surface at regular intervals, but they did nothing to brighten the building's cold, sterile aura. It was the sort of place broken down low level droids went to await recycling.

"This is the place?" I asked.

This is it, said Paige. *Seventeen twelve east Crick avenue. According to the listings, Lars should be on the fourth floor.*

I frowned as I continued to stare.

You're contemplating moving, I can tell.

"No, I'm silently thanking my grandfather for the inheritance—which includes you, Carl, so don't look so glum." My partner sported a grim visage that hinted at Paige's treachery regarding my droid recycling train of thought. Then again, she *had* told me she shared virtually everything with him, like it or not.

I cracked the door and stepped into the Cetie heat. We'd given Lars a call before leaving the office, but he hadn't responded, so I figured we'd try a more personal form of address. I had my doubts about how well we'd fare in our efforts, though.

With Carl on my heels, I approached the residential tower's front door and waited, but the panes of glass stubbornly refused to move.

"What's going on, Paige?" I asked. "Do I need a security code for entry?"

Try the other extreme, she said. *It's manual. You'll have to pull on the handle.*

Carl did the dirty work, holding it open for me to pass through. "No one ever said subsistence on the basic minimum income was glamorous."

Behind the doors, I found a small lobby, populated by a trio of ratty sofa chairs upholstered in a synthetic puke green fabric. A kiosk on the far side, possibly intended for a receptionist, stood empty. A huge pink poster featuring a smiling, greasy-haired used racer salesman sort had been plastered across the bottom of the kiosk, with the words 'Princess Gaming—We Get Gamers!' featured in a bold font. A musty smell hung over the space like a fine mist.

I ignored the lot and headed down a dimly lit hallway, at the end of which I spotted an elevator intermittently illuminated by a flickering light. A panel with a set of buttons was situated on the right-hand side at hand level.

"Let me guess," I said. "No Brain integration?"

What gave it away? said Paige. *The twelve year coat of grime or the rave lighting?*

I punched the up button. After fifteen seconds, a rudimentary chime binged, and the doors opened. I stepped into the lift interior—miraculously free of squatters and foul odors—and queued in the fourth floor. The doors closed once more, the elevator lurched and creaked, and I feared for my life, but thanks to generous factor of safety guidelines implemented by the Cetie Board of Architectural Engineering, I made it to the fourth floor in one piece.

I found Lars's listed apartment under a light that actually functioned properly. Lacking any obvious doorbell, I knocked. Carl and I waited.

I'm taking bets on whether or not he responds, said Paige. *Right now they're fifteen to one against. Better lock your wagers in soon, as those odds will only get worse with time.*

"Seriously, though," said Carl after a minute, "our chances of success here aren't good."

"I know." I eyed a slot in the bottom of the door, roughly the width of a pizza box but three times as high. A scanner had been embedded into the door above it. A pinhead-sized indicator light shone red.

"So why bother coming?" asked Carl.

"Because low odds are not the same as impossible odds," I said. "You go after low hanging fruit first, and in this case, that's visiting Lars directly. Assuming his directory listing is current, coming here could end this case with one swift slice. And again, assuming the listing is correct, he *must* be here. This place is gamer heaven."

And by heaven, I meant a wretched hellhole, but that wouldn't matter to a heavily introverted gaming addict. When a person spent every waking hour in a simulation, what use would they have for decently finished quarters larger than a walk-in closet, or lighting that didn't cut out intermittently, or elevator technology from this millennium? Those would only serve to jack up rents to unreasonable levels. Here, the things that really mattered to gamers seemed to be in place, namely a stout door fitted with an electronically controlled food delivery slot. If I had to guess, should I go digging beneath the building's crumbling concrete and steel, I'd find a fiberoptic bundle providing the lowest latency connection possible to one of the major gaming services—perhaps Princess Gaming, based on the poster downstairs.

Carl knocked again. "I'd be nice if we knew he was here for a fact, though."

"I don't suppose we could triangulate his Brain signal, could we Paige?"

Not unless you obtained a warrant. Oh, and joined the police force first. But if he's a gamer, then a good start would be to identify his avatar name. With that in hand, we could check his online status from the gaming servenets in question. If nothing else, finding out whether or not he's in game would help me update the betting odds I'm offering.

I gave the door a few more seconds. "Alright. Fair enough. Let's see if we can find anyone who might be able to shed some light on this guy."

It was a next to impossible proposition given the lodging, but Carl and Paige were kind enough not to throw it back in my face. After knocking on a few neighbors' doors and getting absolutely nowhere, I headed back to the ground level and approached the lobby kiosk.

It remained stubbornly empty. I slapped the counter and called out. "Hey! Anyone here?"

I startled as a raspy wheeze croaked out from underneath the counter. "No need to shout." *Breathe, clank, wheeze.* "I'm right here."

I looked down and spotted a Meertor perched upon a stool, his respirator covering his eyes, nose, and mouth and the pack that cycled his atmosphere strapped to his back. The top of his head floated several inches shy of the counter, but I doubt I would've noticed him even if he'd been standing. He was abnormally short, even for one of his species.

"What do you need?" he wheezed, his voice muffled by the respirator. "Rooms require only a two hundred SEU deposit. The rest we'll deduct automatically from your monthly government stipend. Very affordable. You'll have plenty to spare for your Princess subscription and food. Although..." His mask shifted toward Carl. "That a droid? Not sure I have any doubles, even if you pony up the deposit."

"Thanks for the offer, but I'm not interested in renting," I said. "Are you the building manager?"

The Meertor shrugged, the skin of his bald scalp wrinkling as he did so. "Close enough. Are you from Compliance? We have the structural engineer's report posted in front. Turns out those cracks in the foundation are nothing to worry about, like we claimed from the start."

I waved my hand. "I'm not with the city. I'm looking for someone. Lars Busk. Name sound familiar?"

Clank. Wheeze. A shake of the head. "Should it?"

"He's a renter here. Apartment four thirty-seven, or so the personal listings claim."

"And you think I'd know him?"

"You work here, don't you?"

The Meertor started to shake, and a gurgling whine emanated from behind his mask. I was halfway up the counter, ready to perform CPR, before I realized removing the respirator would kill him faster than the seizure he was suffering through. Luckily for me, Paige saved me from further embarrassment or any financially debilitating lawsuits.

Relax. He's laughing.

The Meertor quieted and shook his head. "Oh, human. How naïve you are. You think my tenants leave their rooms?"

"You work the front," I said. "You might've remembered when he signed his lease."

"To revisit your previous question, no, I'm not the building manager. And I haven't worked here that long."

"We're getting off track," I said. "The point is, what can you tell me about him?"

The Meertor stood, leaned against the side of the kiosk, and eyed me with suspicion—or so I gathered from his crossed arms and less than stellar posture. I couldn't see his eyes though the mask.

"Who did you say you were?" he wheezed.

"I didn't. Rich Weed. Private investigator. I can Brain you my license."

He nodded, and I obliged. After a moment of what I assumed was intense perusal, he gave me another nod, more comradely this time.

"Seems legitimate," he said, his respirator pack hissing as a valve released. "What did you want to know?"

"Does Lars Busk live here?"

The Meertor settled back onto his chair. "Well, I could check, but I'd have to access the building's servenets. They're encrypted, of course, for our tenants' safety. Not that bypassing it is a problem for me. I have the code, but the encryption service isn't inexpensive. Neither are the building's utility bills, or tax payments..."

I think I understood his drift. "Perhaps if I made a small *donation* to the apartment complex—delivered to you directly for safekeeping—that would make a difference. Say...twenty SEUs?"

The Meertor grunted. "Fifty."

"Thirty-five."

"Deal." The alien tilted his head, likely invoking his Brain. "Apparently, your friend does live here."

"Apartment four thirty-seven?" I asked.

"That's the room he's paying for," wheezed the Meertor.

"Any idea if he's in?"

"He's online, so I assume so."

I was sharp enough to figure out the next question without Paige's prodding. "You're a Princess Gaming affiliate, right? What's Busk's avatar?"

"XXEliteForce420XX."

Lars sounded like a winner. "Any way you could send a message to him in game?"

He responded with another gurgling whine, but just a taste. "As if I'd be friends with any of these hopeless Intros."

I didn't let him off the hook. "I need to contact him. It's about his family."

"So? Send him a Brain missive."

"I did. He won't accept them."

"Probably because he has no interest in speaking to you. How is this difficult to comprehend?"

I felt my anger rising. Paige helped me force it down before I inadvertently sent a foot flying into the alien's head. "Please. I need to relay a message."

The Meertor responded with a long, sad wheeze which I gathered was a sigh. Perhaps the novelty of my presence was wearing off. "You could try some sort of written communicative. But don't ask me to deliver it for you."

"Why not?"

"Because I don't have any interest in getting fired or incarcerated. Most of our tenants are very concerned with privacy. Only a select few entities are authorized to make deliveries to them. Food services, mostly."

"Such as?"

The Meertor made a raspy, gurgling noise and adjusted his respirator.

I think that was the equivalent of him clearing his throat, said Paige.

Wonderful. "Perhaps another donation would help you remember?"

The alien perked. "Thirty-five SEUs?"

I nodded.

The Meertor smiled. "Certainly. I'll send the list of businesses your way."

The inbox in the corner of my vision blinked, so I thanked the clerk and turned toward the door. Carl held it open for me as we poured back out into the Cetie heat.

"Carl," I asked. "Any chance that contract you sent Miss Busk covered incidental expenses?"

"One would think you hadn't lucked into a bonanza of SEUs," he said. "But of course it did. I think of everything."

I smiled. "I'm so glad you do."

So, said Paige as we approached the car. *Should we start our restaurant tour?*

"Soon," I said. "But first, let's drop by the office. There's something I forgot to pick up before we left that might come in handy."

4

The doors to Smotrycz's blinked open upon our approach, hitting Carl and me with a blast of cool, deep-fried air. Molded orange and yellow plastic filled my field of view, along with dozens of holodisplays, regular displays, and plastic statuettes of Donald, the iconic blue-haired, oddly-happy Smotrycz clown. Somewhere in the back fat sizzled and popped, and the air was thick with the smell of tomatoes, spices, and volatilized oil.

A low-level droid in an orange smock greeted us as we approached the service station. "Welcome to Smotrycz's Pies and Fries! Can I interest you in a deep dish soy-cheese and ham pizza or a heaping portion of our famous double-battered fries? Or you could try to beat the heat with one of our signature spicy and refreshing Chili Chillers, now available in Habanero and Datil!"

The bot was an older model, human in appearance but lacking a few key upgrades to its facial response systems. I found its awkward, forced smile that lifted too highly at the corners unnerving. "Uh...no thanks. I was actually hoping I could ask you a question."

"About our menu?" said the droid. "Certainly! I'm well equipped to deal with all your Smotrycz's food and food-like substitute related questions, including information regarding the joule content of our meals, the origins of our sustainably sourced wheat and bacon, and the mercury levels of our farmed halibut."

"*Halibut?*" I said.

"Part of our famous seafood medley pizza, with traditional White™ sauce and your choice of cheese or cheese replacement. Care to order one?"

I was smart enough not to inquire about the rest of the medley. "No, thank you. My question was about delivery."

"Yes, we do deliver!" spouted the droid. "Our drones will happily service any residential or commercial address within a twenty kilometer radius. For locations outside our range, we'd be happy to redirect your order to one of our hundreds of sister locations across Cetie."

"I'm not asking for me," I said. "I'm here for a friend. Lars Busk. I understand you deliver meals to him on a regular basis."

The droid continued to smile, but the slightest of twitches in its cheek indicated I'd thrown it for a loop. "If you're in need of assistance with one of your deliveries, you can call our automated help line. If it's an order originating from our store and you have your order number, I'd be happy to do the same for you here."

I waved Carl forward. I was going to need his help.

"You misunderstand me," I told the droid. "Look. I have a friend. Lars Busk. He receives regular deliveries from you—a medium hand-tossed mushroom and pheasant pie with a side of ginger Snappers, if I'm not mistaken—every ninety-six hours. I need to get ahold of him, but he hasn't been answering my Brain missives. I'm starting to worry."

The droid glanced at Carl. "I'm sorry, sir, but I don't see how this impacts our team at Smotrycz's. If, however, you'd like to order a hand-tossed mushroom and pheasant pizza of your own, I'd—"

"Listen to me," I said. "This man may be in danger. I've tried to contact him via Brain, but he won't respond. The only other option I have is to send him a written message, but due to his living arrangements, I can't get that to him either. Only a few businesses are authorized to deliver to him, and Smotrycz's is one of them. If I'm not mistaken, you'll be sending him his meal soon. All I'm asking is you include a message to him with your delivery." I removed a slim, PolyPly sleeve from my pocket and flashed the slip within at the droid. "Please. I'm not asking a lot."

The droid's brow furrowed—again, in an unnatural, creepy way. He eyed Carl. "Is this true?"

Carl nodded. "I'm afraid so. If there were another method for us to contact him, trust me, we'd pursue it. But the man's family is anxious, and while we're not fully aware of why he's cut off communications with us, there's serious reason for concern."

I held out the card slip engraved with my message to Lars. The droid eyed it, then me, then Carl. Eventually, he reached out a hand and took it.

"This is highly unorthodox," the droid said. "But if you suspect a man may be in danger, which your own droid confirms, then I suppose I'm compelled to aid you in this. I'll include the card with his Smotty Meal."

I pressed my hands together. "Thank you. Really. This means a lot."

The droid eyed me and flashed me another of its awkward grins. "You're...welcome, sir. Now, would you like to place an order?"

I doubted my response would change anything, but no sense in jeopardizing our success. "You bet. Can I get a large side of cheese fries and one of those chillers? Medium sized, but nothing too spicy. Jalapeño flavor, I guess."

"For dine in?"

"No. Take out. Thanks."

The droid provided me with an order number. I paid via Brain and found a seat at a bench in the far corner of the restaurant, behind a couple of stocky Cetieans sharing lunch with a tall Dirax, its mandibles buried deep in a pile of plain, heavily salted fries. Carl sat across from me, shaking his head.

"What is it?" I asked.

Carl glanced at the front of the store, making sure the droid wasn't yet bringing out our meal. "You know what it is. I don't like lying—especially to another droid."

"We didn't lie," I said. "Lars isn't responding to our communications. For all we know, he *could* be in danger. And legally, we're not authorized to make physical deliveries to him, so it's not as if we had any other alternatives."

"We lied by omission," said Carl. "And I'd argue we didn't exhaust our other options. Surely there's a way to ensure Lars sees one of our missives that doesn't involve us violating his personal property and privacy rights, and even if there isn't, we could simply wait. Sooner or later, Lars is going to exit the Brain game he's playing, at which point he'll see the messages we've left him. He may or may not respond, but he'll at least see them. But that's not my biggest problem with what we've done."

"Then what is?"

Carl leveled me with a glare. "Perhaps we didn't *explicitly* lie, but we deliberately manipulated a low-level droid for our benefit. And I was complicit in it! Maybe you don't feel sleazy, but I do."

I opened my mouth to argue, but I didn't have a leg to stand on, mostly because Smotrycz's hadn't been the first restaurant we'd visited. First we'd stopped at Smoothie Maharaja, which according to the data the Meertori desk jockey had provided us with was next in line for delivery to Lars's place. Following that, we tried a run down sandwich shop that followed Smoothie Maharaja on the list, but that too had turned out to be a failure. It wasn't because the data we'd received was inaccurate. Both restaurants *did* deliver to Lars and had deliveries scheduled in the near future, but neither were staffed by the kind of bot I needed.

The smoothie joint's order taker had been too advanced, as fully featured as Carl and with the looks and personality to match. Apparently, the folks at Maharaja valued their customer experience highly. The sandwich shop didn't. Their service station consisted of an interactive kiosk. It wasn't until we reached Smotrycz's that I'd found what I needed. A fully-functional droid, but an older model, a cheaper model—one with all the fundamental droid leanings of human subservience, respect, and trust but without the advanced, non-fast food related computational prowess to determine when a human and android pair were tag-teaming it to their advantage. Because as Carl had hinted, as true as it was that we hadn't lied to the unit, we hadn't been fully honest either.

"Look," I said. "The microbot we concealed in the PolyPly sleeve isn't going to do any harm to Lars. It's a surveillance unit, nothing more."

"But it could," said Carl. "That's my point."

"How?" I asked. "By flying into his eye and poking him with its hundred micron wide lens? Yeah, that'll give his cornea a fierce scratching."

"That's not what I meant," said Carl. "If we're able to conceal something so easily, to deceive so easily, others could do it as well. To ill effect."

"Oh, don't give me this," I said. "Have you forgotten we're trying to reunite a woman with her estranged son? We're the good guys here!"

"So that's it, then?" said Carl. "We've progressed past a point where we care about our methods? The final result is all that matters, regardless of how we get there?"

I waved for him to pipe down. "We can work on recalibrating your moral compass later. Fries and a chiller, ten o'clock."

A server droid rolled over to our table, dropping off my order and thanking us for our patronage. I grabbed the bag and scooted my posterior toward the edge of the bench, but the smell of freshly fried potatoes slathered in processed dairy was too strong. I cracked open the bag, stuffed a few fries in my mouth, and moaned in pleasure. Though a large side of Smotty fries probably contained enough hydrogenated fats to necessitate an early trip to a GenBorn facility for blood refreshment, gosh darn it if those artificial oils didn't burst off the tongue!

"I thought we were leaving," said Carl.

I shrugged and jammed a few more fries in my mouth. "Eh. I'll finish my snack first. Besides, we've got a good eight hours until the package gets delivered if that Meertor didn't steer us wrong. We'll be ready when the time is right."

At least, I hoped we would. I'd never actually tried anything of the sort before. But, hey—what could go wrong?

5

I stood in front of one of my hallway mirrors, eyeing myself from multiple angles. Having just taken a nap and a shower, I patted my hair to make sure the pomade still held firm. As soon as I pulled my hand back, my locks sprang back into place, fresh as a spring hare. *Perfect.*

Vanity, said Paige. *The character or quality of being vain. Possessing excessive pride in one's abilities, appearance—*

Oh, shut it, I told her. *I'm allowed a little self-congratulation every now and then. I happen to think I look darn good for an eighty-five year old former kickboxer.*

You'd look exceptional if this were the year twenty-three thirty, said Paige. *But considering it's a millennia later, I'd say you're a little shy of average.*

You're not going to give me any credit for the straight nose, are you?

I'd be willing to give your reconstructive surgeons credit, perhaps.

I snorted. They'd only restored to me what a few wayward kicks to the face had wrongfully stolen. I turned my head toward the railing. "See anything yet?"

Carl's voice drifted my way from downstairs. "Nothing. Just the inside of the bag. I think we're still in transport."

"And I'm assuming Lars is still online?"

According to the Princess Gaming servenets, he is, said Paige. *Still hasn't responded to any of our Brain missives, before you ask.*

I shook my head. About twelve hours had passed since we first began the investigation, and Lars had yet to sign out. Didn't the guy ever get up to pee?

Don't ask, said Paige.

I headed down my apartment's spiral staircase and joined Carl in the sitting room. My partner sat there on a puffy cerulean sofa set, his feet propped up on an ottoman. I plopped down next to him.

"Paige, let me see," I said.

She obliged. My view of the living room blinked away, replaced by a uniform field of brown so dark it appeared almost black.

"Contrast?" I said.

Sorry, said Paige. *I'll do what I can. We don't have much light in the bag at the moment.*

My vision flared, and I squinted reflexively. The bright flash only lasted a moment as everything quickly settled into a more pleasing spectrum. The resulting image was grainy and indistinct, but at least I could make out the surroundings.

In front of me rose an enormous sheer brown cliff face, several hundred meters tall, its sides bumpy and textured but not enough for me to be able to find purchase. Not that I'd need to. I wasn't really there, having merely switched the visual feed from my own two eyes with the one from the microbot's camera. Though logically I knew I hadn't instantly shrunk down to the width of a human hair, I couldn't help but feel like a gnat's younger, shrimpier cousin—especially once I realized the impossibly tall cliff face in front of me was the side of a Smotrycz's pizza box. Despite the low contrast, I could just make out the right half of an 'm' where it encroached upon the left half of an 'o.'

"How about the other feeds?" I asked. "Scent, sound."

Paige superimposed those over my body's own sensory inputs. A powerful smell of freshly baked bread, ginger, and roasted chicken filled my nostrils, and somewhere in the distance I heard a steady thrumming.

That's the drone's rotary blades, said Paige. *And for the record, that smell is roasted pheasant, not chicken. Please, get it right.*

"My apologies to the planet's poultry farmers," I said. "Do we know how close we are to delivery?"

I heard Carl's voice, though somewhat muffled by the sound of the drone's rotor. "According to the geolocator, we're within a hundred meters of the building. Should be there in no time at all."

"Good," I said. "Now let's cross our fingers and hope Lars's elevator doesn't give out, otherwise this whole food delivery thing will have been a bust."

That won't be a problem, Rich, said Paige. *Even if the elevator fails, we'll be fine.*

"I know," I said. "I have to think like a microbot. Not only does our bot have a set of wings that allow for flight, but even if it didn't, because of its negligible weight, a fall down an elevator shaft wouldn't do any damage, and that's before accounting for the effects of air resistance. Trust me, I'm not an idiot. I'd be more concerned about the drone's ability to get the food up to the delivery slot if that happened."

And I'm glad to know you have a fundamental understanding of the square-cube law, Rich, said Paige. *But the elevator won't be an issue because the building's units have internal and external delivery slots. You didn't notice them set into the exterior windows?*

I hadn't, of course. "Well, there's that, too."

"Approaching the windows," said Carl.

I'm sure the microbot contained a gyroscope as well as several directional accelerometers, so it must've logged the delivery drone's deceleration as it approached Lars's window, but Paige had apparently decided not to simulate those sensations for me—maybe for gastrointestinal purposes. I did, however, hear a tone sound behind the drone's rotating blades, followed by the dull clap of a slot opening. A raspy tear followed, that of hook and loop fasteners. My vision once again faded to white, and I heard a puff and whine of a linear actuator.

Sorry, said Paige. *Looks like we've been pulled from the insulated bag. Fixing contrast again.*

My vision adjusted once more, this time with the end product becoming slightly less fuzzy. Now, in addition to the enormous wall of cardboard, I could make out a white, cloudy barrier surrounding me and looping over the top of the pizza box mountain. A plastic bag, unless I was mistaken.

"I'd guess we're inside the apartment," said Carl, "based on the auditory feed and the geolocation data."

Accelerometers also confirm we've stopped moving, said Paige.

I heard the actuator sound once more, followed by the clap of the slot. The buzzing of the drone blades stopped.

"So we're in?" I said.

"Should be," said Carl.

"Excellent. Paige? Give me the microbot controls."

Uh...you sure about that champ?

"What? You don't trust me?"

If Paige could've gulped, I'm sure she would've. *Do I really need to answer that?*

"Need I remind you I spent several years as a flight-wing instructor?"

"I'm not sure that translates particularly well to microdrone manipulation," said Carl.

"You're not helping my case," I said. "Paige? The controls please."

Fine, she said. *But only because of the aforementioned reasons you already described. Namely that because of basic physics, it's virtually impossible to wreck one of these—virtually being the operative word, so don't go hog wild.*

A pair of joysticks materialized in front of me. I reached out and grabbed them, feeling the triggers with my index and middle fingers and rubbing my thumbs over the numerous small buttons on top.

"Just like on my old flightwing suit," I said. "You're a miracle worker, Paige."

A miracle would've been fabricating the controls out of thin air and attaching them to the bot, said Paige. *I merely superimposed a flightwing control simulation over the microbot's feed. You handle the inputs, and I'll handle translation to something the microbot understands. I figure that's a fair compromise. I also mapped the bot's camera to your head. Give it a try.*

I craned my neck up, and my vision shifted accordingly. "Perfect."

Alright, said Paige. *Let's give it a go then.*

I pushed forward on the joysticks and depressed the topmost triggers. A thrumming sound came to life, probably from the microbot's wings, and I surged into the air. I performed a few quick test loops and paused just to the side of the cardboard cliff face.

Something wrong?

"This doesn't feel right," I told Paige. "I need some flight feedback from the accelerometer data."

This microbot produces some pretty wicked acceleration, Rich, said Paige. *I'm not sure that's a good idea.*

"I never blacked out during flightwing instruction," I said. "If you're that worried, tone it down to a level comparable to what I'm used to."

That's not a bad idea. Fine. Here you go.

I didn't sense any immediate change, but when I pressed forward on the joysticks again, I felt a rush of acceleration. The thrumming of the microbot's wings reverberated through my body.

"Now we're talking," I said. "Let's do this."

With a flick of my wrists, I sailed up the cardboard, the edges of the Smotrycz's lettering rushing up to greet me. I took a line right across the edge of the 'm,' peeling off to the side as I reached the curve at the top of the letter. I twisted as I arrived at the top of the cardboard box, looping onto a horizontal axis and onto the broad expanse of pizza box. With a calm sea of brown beneath me and the gently rippling sky of white from the Smotrycz's bag above me, I increased my speed, air rushing through my hair and my feet trailing a body length from the box's surface.

"This is great," I said. "Remind me to dust off my flightwing suit and take it to the test track some time."

"Or," said Carl, "we could invest in an Iridium™ turbo racer. All the fun of flightwing jaunts and intrastellar joyrides at a fraction of the cost of a space equipped vessel."

"Don't start with me," I said. "I'll spend my money wherever I see fit."

The scene before me shifted. A yawning chasm loomed, beyond which hung only an expanse of white bag. I zoomed right over the edge of the pizza box, diving down into a twist of white plastic at the end of which gleamed a bright hole. With as much speed as I could muster, I exploded out of the twisted ends of the bag and into a sea of color.

Once again my contrast adjusted, this time resulting in a crystal clear image thanks to the bright lighting of the interior of Lars's apartment, but I was too overwhelmed by my surroundings to take much stock in the feed quality.

If I'd felt like a gnat before, then now I felt like a prepubescent aphid. The room stretched around me, its walls impossibly far away, like vistas viewed from the top of a mountain. Lights gleamed at me from high in the sky, a half-dozen suns set into a backdrop of sheet-rock. A calm sea of glossy laminate paneling spread out across the floor, but it was the steep bluff below me that caught my eye.

Dozens of fast food containers, bags, and boxes, piled haphazardly upon one another, some of them seem-ingly untouched, others broken open as new deliveries through the slot had forced the previous ones to the floor. Spilled drinks and melted slushies, upturned piz-zas and deconstructed burgers. The sheer size was overwhelming, reminiscent of a child's fanciful bedtime story or a fat kid's worst nightmare.

Our own most recent delivery sat atop the pile—a pizza plateau if you will. Lars's drink order had tipped on its side upon entry, sending its contents pouring through a straw and onto the scene underneath. The resulting soda river poured over a jagged peak of French fry monoliths before snaking around burger basin and into the stir-fry swamps.

I wriggled my nose in response to the smells being fed to me. I think the microbot's sensors were more finely tuned than my own olfactory systems.

"Am I the only one detecting a certain...*fragrance* here?" I asked.

Apparently Carl had been patched through into the same feeds I had. "There's definitely something pun-gent in the air. Certainly, this pile hasn't been touched in a while. Maybe two or three weeks, based on the size. Depends on Lars's daily calorie intake."

I'd say three, said Paige, *based on the flavored churro sampler poking out of the mass near the floor. If the Meertor's data can be believed, those are a once a month sort of thing.*

That much wasted food wasn't a good sign. It indicated Lars might've jumped ship without anyone being the wiser—but if so, why would his estranged mother have come looking for him at roughly the same moment? Perhaps there was more to the case than I'd initially been led to believe.

I spun in mid air, taking note of the barest essentials of a kitchenette, a microwave and fridge, far off in the corner of the room. Besides that, I spotted a dining table decorated with a single chair, a flimsy cot, and a toilet with corresponding washbasin. No sign of Lars, though.

Don't lose faith, said Paige. *It's not a studio. Try the door.*

Paige highlighted the entryway in question. I pushed forward on the joysticks, zooming through the air at top speed as I raced toward the barrier. The door stood closed, but at my current size, it posed no impediment at all. I zipped underneath it, through the gap between door and floor, which to me seemed a yawning chasm. If only entry into Lars's apartment had been so simple, but despite its shoddy construction, each unit in Lars's building had been hermetically sealed. Intros took their privacy seriously.

My contrast once again adjusted as I entered the new room, this one lacking a window but with a pair of mood lights painting the room in a dim, earthy glow. A single piece of furniture populated the space—an enormous padded black lounge chair, with the back tilted to a forty-five degree angle. It stood on a wide base, seemingly affixed to the floor. The words 'Princess Gaming' stretched across the side of it in bright pink.

Remember how you wondered about Lars's bathroom habits, and I said not to ask? said Paige. *Well, that's how. A top of the line Princess Gaming rig. It's not just a comfy place to lay while playing Brain games. It contains hard-wired fiber optic access to the Princess servenets, as well as aqueous infusers, climate controls, and internal plumbing. For gamers, it doesn't get much better than this.*

The unit faced the wall, so I couldn't see much more than its back and sides. I zoomed forward, the thrum of the wings echoing through my body. Wind whistled through my hair and into my nostrils.

The latter took note. "Am I the only one who smells that?"

The fetid stink from the food hadn't gone away. If anything, it had intensified.

"I have a bad feeling about this, Rich," said Carl.

I rounded the edge of the Princess chair and received my first view of Lars. He roughly matched the image we'd sourced for him from the public listings, with light brown hair, a bit of a baby face, and a nose that matched his mother's. He sported a scraggly beard and long, unkempt hair, which I didn't find abnormal for an Intro of his caliber, but given the quantity of food in his apartment, I hadn't expected for him to be so thin and frail.

Of course, I also hadn't expected for his eyes to be sunken, his skin to be waxy and discolored, and for a putrid stench of decomposition to roll off of him.

"Uh, Paige..." I said. "I think it's time we call the police."

6

I stared at the doorway between the main portion of Lars's apartment and his gaming room. Somewhere from within the confines of the gaming quarters, I heard the light whirr of a quartet of drone rotors—not from a delivery bot this time, but from one of the police units recording the scene.

A throat was forcefully cleared, and I turned my attention back to the uniformed officer in front of me. Oliver Sanz, or so his lapel tag indicated—tall and dark-skinned with a crisp high top fade, dressed in the traditional baby blue and beige of Cetie's enforcers of the law. He seemed impossibly close, and the walls of the apartment loomed over me like those of a jail cell.

It was the microbot's fault. After a jaunt through its eyes, Lars's previously cavernous apartment now induced in me a sense of claustrophobia.

"So," said Sanz, his arms crossed. "Explain to me the situation one more time. From the beginning, if you could."

"I already explained it," I said. "Don't you guys record every witness interaction? Why do you need me to tell you the same thing twice?"

"In case you *fail* to tell me the same thing twice," said Sanz. "Now talk. Before I decide to make you repeat yourself a third time."

I wrinkled my nose and frowned, but the nasal twitch wasn't entirely due to Sanz's attitude. The lone window in Lars's apartment had been forced open, and the front door had been locked into place at its maximum operational width, but the lingering funk hadn't dissipated in the least. Supposedly, the mind filtered out omnipresent odors after a while, but apparently the stink of death was too strong an indicator for the mind to relegate to its far reaches.

I could shut off information from your nose's mitral cells, if you like, said Paige.

"Look," I said, ignoring Paige. "I already told you what happened. A woman by the name of Helena Busk, who claimed to be Lars Busk's estranged mother, hired me to track down her son who she hadn't been able to contact via Brain in some time. The case seemed fairly straightforward. We found Lars's physical address in the personal listings. Unfortunately, contacting Lars wasn't as easy as we'd hoped. He was as unwilling to answer our Brain missives as his mother's—because, as it turns out, he was dead."

"Right," said Sanz. "But let's return to you, shall we? You came to his apartment. Tried to rouse him, correct? Then you knocked on some doors, again without success, and talked to the Meertori manager downstairs."

"That's right," I said. "Nice fellow. Creepy laugh, but nice nonetheless."

"And then?"

"What do you mean, *and then*?" I said. "I told you. We set up some surveillance. Tracked his online presence. That sort of thing."

"That's a rather vague statement."

I shrugged.

Officer Sanz lifted an eyebrow. "The Meertor said he received an *anonymous tip* about Mr. Busk's passing."

"And a good thing, too," I said. "Otherwise the smell might've soon become unbearable to his neighbors. On second thought, perhaps that's who provided the tip."

Sanz tapped his fingers against his arm. "Look, Mr. Weed. I feel I should mention that we're happy *someone* came through with the tip, but we'd be happier if we knew who it was, simply so we knew how the knowledge had been gained. And if said knowledge was obtained through some breach of privacy...well, I imagine it could be overlooked so long as the motives behind said action didn't have anything to do with Mr. Busk's death. Do I make myself clear?"

I nodded. "I'll be sure to keep that in mind. Thanks."

I heard footsteps and turned to find an EMT entering the premises, a collapsible gurney held under one arm. Given Lars's state, I didn't think the technician would have a hard time moving the body on her own, but wheeling the gurney around in the apartment's tight confines might prove to be a bigger problem.

She disappeared into the dedicated gaming room, and I turned back to Officer Sanz. "Can I ask you something?"

"You can ask," he said. "I may or may not answer. You know how active investigations go—I hope."

The sharp clack of the gurney extending to full size trickled around the corner.

"Don't you find it odd Lars was online at the time of his death?" I asked. "Well, maybe not right *at* his time of death. But my investigation showed him signed into his Princess Gaming account earlier today. He's clearly been dead for weeks. In fact—"

Paige, could you check on Lars's status?

You mean XXEliteForce420XX? she said. *Sure. Let's see. Yeah. He's still online.*

"—according to Princess Gaming's servenets, he's still online."

"It's probably a glitch on Princess's side," said Sanz. "I wouldn't worry about it."

I heard a feminine voice curse, followed by a grunt, a thump, and a squeaky creak, again from the direction of the gaming room.

Actually, scratch that, said Paige. *He's gone offline.*

I glanced in the direction of the noise, a befuddled look on my face.

Sanz must've noticed. "Let me guess. He just disappeared?"

I nodded.

"Told you," said Sanz. "Sometimes these gaming rigs that are directly plugged into the provider's servenets can mess things up. If people die while in the rigs, it can think they're still online. Happens because the Brain has a hard-wired link though which residual power can transfer. Creepy, but I've seen it happen before."

"You have?"

Sanz shrugged. "Where do you think is the most likely spot for an Intro gamer to kick the bucket?"

"Makes sense." I stood there chewing on my lip and knitting my eyebrows.

"You're free to go, by the way," said Sanz. "But think about what I told you. If it turns out there was any foul play here, you could make your life a whole lot easier by coming clean now."

"You mean the anonymous *tipster* could make *their* life easier by coming clean."

Sanz snorted. "Yeah."

I about-faced and walked into the fourth floor hallway of Lars's apartment building. Carl waited for me at the end of the hallway.

"How'd it go?" he asked.

"Didn't Paige relay my Brain feed to you?" I depressed the down button.

"It's called conversation. Don't ruin it."

I smiled. "It was alright. Officer Sanz isn't a dummy. Best that you stayed away."

Not that Carl wouldn't, or *couldn't,* lie for me, but he preferred not to. Having to choose between loyalty and subservience to me, his master, and an officer of the peace gave him the robotic equivalent of heartburn.

The elevator chimed, and we both stepped in.

"I wonder how we'll break the news to Helena," said Carl as the door closed.

"I was thinking we'd hold off on that," I said. "At least for the moment."

Carl looked at me aghast. "You can't be serious? She deserves to know."

"Agreed," I said. "And I'm not suggesting we should deceive her or hide the information from her. Buy I first want to make sure the man we found in there is actually Lars Busk."

Carl blinked. "I'm not sure I follow. The man in that gaming rig looked an awful lot like the photographs of Busk we found in the civilian registries, if admittedly more unkempt."

The elevator dinged again and we both stepped out into the first floor hallway. "Yes, Carl, I know that. And believe it or not, my first instinct isn't that we're dealing with a doppelganger of some sort. But I find it highly suspicious Lars was signed into his Princess Gaming account until the moment his body was removed from his rig."

"I take it you don't buy Officer Sanz's glitch explanation?"

I shrugged. "I suppose it's possible. But remember—we sent him Brain missives, too. They weren't turned away. They went through. Right, Paige?"

Correct, boss, she said.

"And I find it highly unlikely that Princess Gaming's servenets and Cetie's own public servenets *both* suffered similar, concurrent glitches," I said.

Carl smiled and shook his head.

"This is funny to you somehow?" I asked.

"No, I simply suffered a sneaking suspicion you wouldn't drop this case despite Lars's apparent death. Guess I was right."

"And by sneaking suspicion, I don't suppose you actually meant a bet with Paige?"

Carl's mouth opened. "What? I—"

Blame me, not him, she said. *It was my idea.*

"What did the bet entail?" I asked.

It was about your spaceship fetish and what course of action to take, said Paige. *Seriously, don't sweat it.*

"Promise me one thing, though," said Carl.

"Yes?"

"If it turns out you're wrong about Lars, we tell Miss Busk straight away, and we don't charge her for the spurious inquiry."

"Please," I said. "Bilking grieving widows isn't part of my business platform. Neither is being an insensitive jerk. We'll tell her as gently as we can, but we also have a duty to be as thorough and certain of ourselves as possible, which means being a hundred percent certain of Lars's demise and the cause thereof. So let's get to work. We owe it to Helena."

7

I settled into a comfortable sofa chair in my sitting room and propped my feet up on an ottoman, talking to myself as I did so. "Alright. Full belly? Check. Hydrated? Check. Bladder? Recently expressed. Well-rested? Close enough. I think I'm good to go."

This isn't as if you're preparing for a weeks long expedition into the desert, or taking a one man submarine ride into the depths of Cetie's oceans, said Paige. *You're simply signing onto a gaming service for crying out loud.*

"Better to be prepared than not," I said. "I may not be a gamer myself, but I know how they roll. I could be in there for hours, and unlike Lars, I haven't invested in a rig that takes care of my body's fluid inputs and outputs for me."

We could probably whip one up if you so desired, said Paige. *All we'd really need is a bucket and some tubing.*

I grimaced. "Yeah, how about you remind me to head out of the simulation in a few hours in the event I get too immersed."

I guess that works, said Paige. *But don't expect to ever climb the competitive gaming ranks with that attitude.*

Carl sauntered by and helped himself to a seat on the couch opposite me. "So. I heard you're ready to go in."

"Sure am," I replied. "What about you? Are you fully charged? Did you grease your actuators? Did you...I don't know. What else do you do to keep yourself in peak physical condition?"

"Nothing," said Carl. "It's one of the benefits of not being biological. But I'm not coming with you."

"What?" I said. "Paige, did you forget to buy Carl his own subscription? Seriously, they're not that expensive."

"Cost isn't the factor," said Carl. "Once again, it's biology. They won't let me play."

I blinked. "What do you mean? Why not?"

There are a few reasons, said Paige. *The first and foremost is precisely because of those gaming ladders I alluded to. Gaming is competitive, and droids are simply faster than humans. Their physical speed and dexterity don't matter in a simulation, but the mental aspects do, and that's where the disparity between organic and synthetic life is the most glaring. If you let droids compete in gaming tournaments, humans would never win. Easier to ban them outright.*

"And the other reasons?" I asked.

They're interpersonal and sociological, mostly, said Paige. *While Intros can find face to face interactions almost crippling, most are extremely sociable in simulated contexts. That's actually one of the major draws of gaming services such as Princess's. Studies show gamers spend roughly equal time in games as they do in the simulated hub worlds.*

"What does this have to do with androids?" I asked.

"When individuals sign on to a gaming service, they want to know the people they're interacting with are actually *people*," said Carl. "If they were to find out their best friends were actually droids in real life, they'd feel cheated. It's stereotypical and quite frankly hurtful, but to most gamers, droids are no different than NPCs."

"I don't speak gamer," I said. "Someone's going to have to translate."

Non-player characters, said Paige. *Simulated consciousnesses. Like me, basically, but not as much fun.*

I snorted. "Who could be? But seriously, that means you're not joining me in the gaming sim, Carl?"

He shook his head. "Wish I could, Rich. But I'll keep a good eye on you from here in the real world. Make sure the mice don't nibble on your toes."

Don't worry, said Paige. *I'll be there with you, right at your side.*

"Of course you will," I said. "It's impossible to shake you. You're like a drug-resistant fungal infection."

Kisses. Love you too.

"Okay, let's go over the plan," I said. "We'll sign in and focus on finding the folks who show up in Lars's friend list and recently played list. Hopefully, either they'll be able to confirm Lars hasn't been online in weeks, in which case we can assume his account was in fact glitched, or they'll tell us otherwise, and we can play it from there. Paige? What does Lars's Princess account list as his most recently played game?"

Marked 4 Death, said Paige. *It's an acclaimed zombie shooter. It's said to be very lifelike, assuming you can buy into the physically impossible concept of zombies in the first place.*

"Well, it's a trope to be sure," I said. "But given the levels of genetic engineering we've achieved, I'd hesitate to say anything's *impossible*..."

I don't mean it in a biological sense, said Paige. *I mean that zombies couldn't function without breaking fundamental laws of thermodynamics. Seriously. They don't eat, except for the odd brain or two. Given the joule demands of the human body, and one would assume the undead one, zombies would quickly shrivel and cease to function. Anyone trapped in a zombie apocalypse could simply wait for a few weeks in a bunker and emerge to find all the undead impotent. Maybe if they photosynthesized, but seeing as they spend most of their time shambling around at night...*

Good thing I wasn't a horror addict, otherwise my spirits would've been forever crushed. "Forget I ever asked. Are any of Lars's friends still playing Marked 4 Death?"

Paige checked the gaming servenets for me. *Looks like two of them are currently signed in, in a party no less, which makes our task a bit simpler.*

"Can we track them?"

I'm not sure, said Paige. *I've never played the game either, having resided in your head for the past, you know, ever. But as far as I know, Princess is like any other online gaming service in that they offer in-game player tracking and data. Remember, they want to engage people socially. It's a huge part of their draw.*

"Perfect," I said. "So that's where we'll go. Paige. Are we ready?"

Again, it's not as if we're preparing for a high speed take-off. You give the word, and I'll sign you in.

"Well, let's do it, then," I said. "Carl. See you on the flip side."

Carl gave me a nod and a smile as my vision faded to black.

8

A scene materialized in front of me, a flat sea of pink with the words 'Princess Gaming—We Get Gamers!' floating before my eyes in a large white font. That soon faded, replaced by a circular room, but one no less pink than the indistinct ocean of color that had preceded it. The carpeting, walls, and ceiling had all been pulled from a baby girl's nursery, as had the upholstery on the pair of sofa chairs in front of me. On first glance, there didn't appear to be any exits, merely an enormous display on the far wall, one unsurprisingly trimmed in bubblegum pink.

"Well, this is a little nice for a dilapidated zombie shack," I said. "But I guess I'll take it. I've never been particularly into the whole blood and guts scene."

"It's the mandatory new signee orientation," said Paige. "We won't be able to enter Marked 4 Death until we complete it. Should be pretty painless."

"Speaking of pain, how lifelike are these games anyway?" I asked. "If a zombie latches onto my arm and starts chowing down, will I be blinded by searing agony?"

"Relax, Rich," said Paige. "These are games, first and foremost. You can engage a realism mode if you so desire, but most don't. Try to enjoy yourself."

I felt a touch on my shoulder. I whirled and screamed, fists ready for action.

"Seriously?" said Paige. "If you're acting like this now, I can't wait until we get in the game."

Paige stood behind me, exactly as I'd always imagined her—roughly my height, strong and slender, with skin the color of caramel, spiky black hair, and piercing green eyes flecked by blue and gold. A pair of pinkish, purplish blue space-themed leggings hugged her lower body, while a plain black tank top revealed her well-toned arms.

"You're...here," I said dumbly.

"Yeah," she said. "One of the benefits of getting to tag along with you into a virtual world. I actually get a body. What do you think?"

Paige crossed her feet, stuck out a hand, and performed a little twirl, but the room's pink carpeting and the high-top sneakers she wore weren't designed for low friction. She petered out before she completed her three-sixty.

"I think you need to work on your dance moves, is what I think," I said.

Paige gave me a long glance over the end of her nose. "I spend decades inside your head before showing myself, and that's the best you've got? No wonder you're single."

"So let me get this straight," I said. "Carl can't sign into the gaming servenets, but you can? What's the logic there?"

"I'm only here because you are," said Paige. "I couldn't sign on by myself, avoiding that human or not human, player or non-player character sticking point we already discussed."

"Seems like a thin line to toe," I said. "Especially given your non-threatening, nerdacious good looks. You'll be beating them off with a stick, if given the chance."

"Well, thank you," said Paige with a small courtesy. "But I wouldn't worry too much about that. As a function of your Brain, I won't show up in the gaming metadata. Other players will be able to see me and interact with me, but they'll all know exactly what I am—which may reflect poorly on you, so be prepared."

"What? Why?"

"Gaming with your Brain avatar?" Paige tilted her head and gave me a smirk. "Kind of a noob thing to do."

I heard the wail of guitars and the thrum of a bass behind me. I turned, finding that the large, wall-mounted display had flared to life. A promotional vid of some sort had started to play, one featuring clips of various games—hundreds of fighters zipping through space exchanging pulse rounds and firing torpedoes, a knight in shining armor riding a dragon into a wall of flame, and a dark corridor with flashing lights and ominous rumbles echoing forth, among others. After a minute, the clips ended, as did the promotional jingle, instead being replaced with the now familiar Princess Gaming logo.

The logo receded to a backdrop, and a man walked out on screen, the same greasy-haired, grey-suit clad salesman type I'd seen on the poster in the lobby of Lars's apartment building.

"Hello, gaming fan," he said, giving me the finger guns, "I'm Johnny Masters, president and CEO of Princess Gaming, where *we get gamers*. Looking to escape the monotony of everyday life? To engage in fierce battles with everything from rogue Diraxi overlords to all-powerful necromancers? To explore the vast expanse of space at a speed physics can only dream to match? Or perhaps, like myself, you're a lifelong introvert looking for social engagement with your peers in a casual, stress-free environment?

"Well, you've come to the right place. Princess Gaming is Cetie's industry leader in fully immersive Brain gaming, with over ten thousand exclusive games and simulations, over ten billion square kilometers of actively maintained hub worlds, and tens of millions of subscribers. Whether it's action, fantasy, science fiction, horror, adventure, or simply social interaction you're after, you'll find it here at Princess! And I don't say that as merely the president of Princess Gaming, but as an active gamer, member, and contributor to the Princess community myself. So let me be the first to thank you for your decision to join our thriving world, and remember—when you're in a Princess sim, the only rule is to *have fun!*"

The display flicked off, and the entire unit began to fold upon a hinge toward the ceiling.

I shook my head. "Princess Gaming. What kind of name is that anyway? Did they initially have trouble appealing to the female market?"

"It's an old gaming trope," said Paige. "*The princess is in another castle.* It's from one of the very first video games of all time."

A beam of light sliced through the wall below the now retracted display. It opened, like a portal into another universe. I walked forward, but before I'd taken two steps, a couple had emerged from the glowing rectangle. One was a stunningly beautiful woman with a Gaian build, long blonde hair, and a tight, three-piece skirt suit. The other was more familiar.

"Hey," I said. "You're the guy from the vid."

"That's right," he said as he approached. "Johnny Masters. Pleasure to meet you."

He stuck out a hand. I reluctantly shook it. Thankfully, it wasn't as greasy as his hair.

"Rich Weed," I said. "No offense, but can I, you know...play some games now?"

Masters smiled. "Ah, a man after my own heart. Don't worry, friend. That'll come soon enough. But as president and CEO of Princess Gaming, I place the utmost importance on our user experience, which is why I *personally* greet every new enrollee in our services to thank them—and to familiarize them with our in game controls and terms of operation so that each and every one experiences a safe, comfortable, and enjoyable time while here at Princess."

Paige snorted.

Masters smiled even more broadly and extended his hand to her. "Johnny Masters. You are?"

She didn't shake. "Bernadette P. Floppypants. President and CEO of Rich's gray matter."

"That's Paige," I said. "She runs my Brain."

"A little on the facetious side, I take it," said Masters.

"Me?" said Paige. "*Never*. But when you introduced yourself as *the* Johnny Masters, I assumed we'd already entered one of Princess's various fantasy lands. You know, seeing as it would be impossible for you to *personally* greet the hundreds of new gamers who join your service every hour, and that a real CEO would have much better things to waste his time on than meet and greets."

Masters spread his arms out wide, never faltering in his smile. "You see right though me, Paige. If you wish to be technical about it, I'm Mr. Masters' personal avatar, but I assure you, for all intents and purposes, I am him and he is me. Our company engineers worked tirelessly to ensure that my real and digital personas matched *perfectly*. Why? Because *we get gamers,* that's why! And at Princess, we want to ensure that every interaction, whether it be with another life form or a digital consciousness imprint such as yourself is as flawless as possible. Now, Mr. Weed, if you wouldn't mind, let's go ahead and proceed with the orientation. Let's start with a simple spatial coordinates exam to ensure your Brain's compatibility with our systems. Simply move your arms forward, up, and to the sides concurrently, and when you're done with that, please tilt your head up, down, and side to side."

"Seriously?" I said. "Look, I may not be a regular gamer, but it's not as if I've never jumped into a sim before."

"All part of the orientation, Mr. Weed," said Masters. "The faster we get through it, the faster you can get to gaming. Besides, as I already said, your safety and enjoyment is of utmost concern to us. By testing—"

I held up a hand. "Look, I know how this works. Isn't there a waiver I could sign? You know, saying that if I get stuck in a wall it's my own fault because I didn't sit through your lousy seminar? Or that if I suffer night terrors from playing too much Marked 4 Death I won't consider you responsible?"

"Very well." Masters snapped at the woman who stood by his side. She produced a small, portable display from behind her back and gave it to him. He tapped a few buttons before holding it forward.

A mass of text filled the screen. Masters pointed to a box in the lower right hand corner. "To affirm you were offered the orientation training and refused, please press your thumb here."

I did so.

Masters tapped a few more buttons and held the screen forth again. "And to absolve Princess Gaming of liability in the use of our gaming services, including gross negligence on the part of you, the user, and glitches, malfunctions, and errors on the part of us, Princess Gaming, and covering everything from damage to Brains and associated computing systems, physical disease, malnourishment, and sloth resulting from excessive consumption of Princess services, and psychological damage induced by participation in any number of lifelike Princess simulations, please press your thumb here."

Again, I did so. "Is that it?"

Masters snapped the screen back and held it between hands clasped at his waist. "That's it, Mr. Weed. I hope you enjoy your time with us for as long or short as it may be. And remember—should you change your mind, you can always retake this orientation from within your internal hub. Just pull up your visual overlay to access it."

Masters stepped to the side, as did the smartly dressed hostess. He extended his hand toward the portal. I took a step towards it.

"And Mr. Weed?"

I paused and sighed. "Yes...?"

Masters gave me the finger guns. "Remember. Have fun!"

"I'll try."

I gestured to Paige and stepped through the portal.

I'm not entirely sure what I expected—to fall though a parti-colored wormhole, feel a rush of acceleration, or have my surroundings pixelate, dissipate, and coalesce into something new—but the experience was more like passing under a white drape. Suddenly, the pink of the orientation room was gone, replaced with a dilapidated living room, one with moldy walls, boarded windows, filled with moth-eaten furniture, and covered in a thin layer of grime. A single antique lamp set upon an end table tried its hardest to fill the room with light, but its weak rays faded and disappeared as they made their way toward the room's high ceiling and up the warped wooden staircase at my back. Overall, the dwelling seemed ancient and backwards, but I supposed part of the appeal of horror games was a certain rustic, minimalist *je ne sais quoi.*

Paige stepped through the portal and joined me at my side, after which the floating white rectangle winked and disappeared.

"Looking good, Rich," she said.

"Huh?" I looked down. "Gah!"

Somehow I'd lost my lightweight guayabera and Linenesse slacks combination, which had been replaced with a pair of worn cargo pants and a stained white tank top. My pant hems had been stuffed into the black combat boots I wore, and a heavy flack jacket rested upon my chest.

I gave Paige a look. "How did this happen? And why didn't you suffer the same fate?"

Paige still rocked her leggings and tight, sleeveless top, though there was a new addition. A bandolier packed with a half-dozen shells hung over her torso, and peeking over her shoulder were the butt and stock of a weapon—a shotgun, if the shells were any indication.

"I was already prepared for the apocalypse," she said. "Tight fitting clothes and running shoes, baby. That's all you need. Besides, you look good in camo and riot gear. You're like a sexy space marine turned dad turned man who doesn't know how to launder his clothes."

"Um...thanks?" I reached over my shoulder for my own firearm. My fingers found the smooth wooden handle, but when I pulled, rather than the rustle of fabric and the clank of gun components, I heard a ring.

I looked down at my hand. "A *machete*? How come you get a shotgun and I get a machete?"

"You were expecting a Gauss rifle with optional chainsaw attachment?" Paige drew her weapon. "This is the first time we've signed in. You're level one. A machete is standard fare. We're fighting zombies, after all."

"You got a shotgun..." I said.

"Yeah. With—" She glanced at her bandolier and cracked her barrel. "—a whopping six shells. Want to trade?"

The light flickered, and I heard a moan, followed shortly by a loud wooden creak. I tried to turn toward the sound, but I found I wasn't sure where it had come from. The stairs? Down the hallway? Over by the windows?

"That's okay, " I said. "You can..."

Keep it, is what I'd meant to say, but the words stuck in my craw at the sight of the undead terror lurking in the shadows at the edge of my vision.

9

The zombie lunged at me with surprising speed, its face a mass of purple, rotting flesh, with one eye missing and a gaping hole in one of its cheeks. Its mouth yawned as it flew toward me, flashing me a handful of yellow teeth.

I danced back and slashed with my machete, catching the zombie's extended right arm across the hand. Fingers sloughed off and twirled through the air, trailed by thin streams of blood and ichor, but the zombie barreled forth, undeterred. I caught it further up the arm with my return stroke, hearing a wet crack of broken bones and sending more foul blood spraying into the air.

None of it mattered. The zombie plowed toward me as if it had been bitten by an ant, reaching for me with its mauled arm and good one alike.

On a conscious level, I panicked, but my years of professional kickboxer training held firm. As the zombie closed, I pivoted and twirled, sending the heel of my boot into the creature's unprotected head. A shudder went down my leg as the skull crunched, and the zombie dropped to the floor like a bag of wet sand.

I raised my machete high, eying the zombie for movement.

"Finish it!" said Paige.

She leveled the shotgun at the reanimated corpse, the weapon's butt firmly pressed into her shoulder and her right eye aligned along the sights.

"I think it's—"

It groaned and swiped an arm at my leg. I yelped and brought the machete crashing down on its neck, severing head from body. Foul smelling viscera sprayed across my pants.

I looked up at Paige and scowled. "Thanks for the help."

"Better save that apology and issue me a real one in a few minutes."

"For what?" I asked.

A loud crash sounded from the direction of the windows. Cracked boards clattered to the ground as decaying, diseased arms pushed through them, thrashing and clawing wildly. Moans and throaty growls poured in though the gaps, as they did from down the depths of the dark hallway.

"For saving my shells," she said. "Quick. Up the stairs."

I turned and mounted the steps, the boards creaking under my feet. I made it halfway to the second floor before a trio of discolored corpses careened around the corner at the top, fighting each other and grasping at the topmost banister for purchase.

A sharp crack spilt the air. The zombies collapsed and toppled down the stairs, their heads turned to jelly.

"Five left," said Paige as she passed me by, cramming another shell into her barrel. "We need a room we can barricade. Quick!"

The roar from downstairs intensified as I reached the top of the steps, and I heard the thump of heavy feet. A zombie roared and lunged at me. I lopped off half its jaw with a swipe of my machete and kicked the rest of it down the stairs. Paige's shotgun rent the air again, followed by the thump of several more bodies hitting the hardwood.

"Four!"

"In here!" I said.

I dashed into the only room I could see with a working light source, a small bathroom in desperate need of a thorough cleaning. I ripped the shower curtain from its bar, my machete held at the ready, but the tub was empty of anything except lime scale. Paige slammed the door shut behind us, flicking a button on the door handle to lock it.

The first zombie slammed against it almost instantaneously, rattling the door in its frame.

"Now what?" asked Paige.

"How should I know?" I said. "You're the one who's apparently well versed in zombie fighting tactics."

"It's called conserving ammo," said Paige. "Shotguns are for crowd control. Isn't that obvious?"

The door shuddered again. Something moaned, and a hand burst through the flimsy wood, the splinters raking bloody trails along the undead arm.

I shrieked and lashed out with my brush trimmer turned zombie whacker, severing the arm at the elbow with a wet crunch. The liberated arm thumped as it fell to the ground, blood splattering across the grimy subway tile, the fingers still twitching. Though I knew in the conscious, logical part of my mind that I was in the middle of a simulation, my stomach wasn't so easily convinced. It turned, and I tasted bile.

I forced my snack back down through sheer force of will, the smell of the shambler's rotting flesh causing me to reel. "Urgh...I think I could do with a little less realism, at least with respect to my non-visual sensory organs."

Zombies groaned, and the door rattled. Paige stuck the muzzle of her gun in the gap left by the zombie's overreach and cut loose. A concussive blast rent the air, leaving a mist of sulfurous spent powder in its wake.

"We'll change the settings later," said Paige. "No time now. Secure the door!"

I wasn't sure how she expected me to do that, but I did what I could with my limited resources. I grabbed the shower curtain rod with curtain still attached and jammed it diagonally across the closed door, forcing one end into the sheetrock. Then I tipped a free-standing linen closet across the door in the opposite direction, closing off the hole created by the grabby zombie and hopefully stalling him and his buddies.

Of course, I'd also blockaded us in the bathroom. Luckily, Paige was on the ball. I turned to find her at a window, methodically knocking free boards that had been nailed over it with the butt of her gun.

Whack. Whack. Whack. One of the boards rattled, and a nail fell out. Paige dug her fingernails under the edge and began to pry.

She looked at me over her shoulder as she tugged. "Well? Do something. Either help with the window or look for supplies."

"*Supplies?*" I said. "It's a bathroom."

"You'd be surprised." Paige nodded toward the mirror.

I had to remind myself of the game's archaic setting and the likely building architecture. I pushed on the corner of the mirror to no effect, but when I pulled on it, it swung open. Inside, I found a small cabinet, on one shelf of which was a small plastic bottle and on another a mysterious white box with a red cross on it.

"You've got to be kidding me," I said. "Painkillers and...what is this? A med pack?"

"It's a persistent trope for a reason," said Paige as another board clattered to the floor. "Real medical care is slow, painful, and a drag on the action. Besides, we're in a genre game. You can't introduce modern medical procedures. It would ruin the ambiance."

The zombies moaned and beat on the door, but they didn't seem to be making any progress against the cabinet.

I grabbed the pills and mysterious box. "You'd think people would rather play something new and different in the horror genre. This? It's stale."

"And some folks do," said Paige. "But that's not what you get in Marked 4 Death. Put the pair in your inventory for later."

I glanced down at my camo pants, trying to figure out which pocket was best suited for the task.

"No, genius," said Paige. "Your inventory, not your pockets."

"I heard you the first time." I kept staring. "But I'm finding I, ah...don't know how to do that."

Paige sighed. "I knew we'd regret skipping the new player orientation." The door rattled and shook, and a new chorus of moans started up. "Just stick them in your pants. I'll show you in a moment."

Paige pulled off another board and knocked the last one loose with a few more targeted strikes. Somehow, the window behind the wooden planks was still in one piece, so Paige flipped the latch, pushed it up, and motioned me over.

"Want to go first?" she said.

I cast my gaze into the abyss. I couldn't see a thing. "This is the second floor, right?"

"I think so," said Paige. "Are you worried about turning an ankle?"

"Are you kidding?" I said. "I've got a med pack. I'll be fine."

I readied myself at the sill, machete still gripped in my right fist. Jumping out a second story window with a sharp, forty-five centimeter piece of steel in my hand perhaps wasn't the best idea, but I did it anyway. Better to suffer an ignominious death by impalement than be torn to shred by zombies, in my eyes.

I needn't have worried. I hit the ground lightly, with the machete held out of harm's way. Another light thump followed me, that of Paige's feet hitting the damp soil. As my eyes adjusted, no longer blinded by the comparatively bright light of the grime-covered wash closet, I made out Paige's outline as well as the dull siding of the house. Behind me, bulbous, leafy trees loomed like giants over dark fields of some thick, tall crop—possibly corn. Clouds crept across the sky, blotting out whatever light the stars and moons provided.

Moans and thumps continued to echo out from the open window above us, but no sounds of life or any twisted, undead facsimile thereof wandered over from the surrounding undergrowth.

I shuffled over to Paige and spoke in a low voice, just in case. "So...what now? How do we find Lars's former party? Does this game have an internal map system?"

Paige reached over and tapped the side of my forehead twice. In response to her touch, a Brain display appeared over my vision, including an empty inventory display, a health bar, a compass, and a minimap.

"I just engaged your HUD," said Paige, "which you would've known how to do if you'd bothered to sit and listen to Johnny Masters' spiel. You should have a mini map, but you can access the main one through regular Brain controls. You asked about inventory? Activate it, then handle the painkillers and med pack. They'll digitize, and you'll see them on your display. You'll be able to do the same with ammo, but not weapons. With those, you only keep what you can carry."

"Perfect," I said, bringing up the main map. "So where do we find Lars's crew?"

"If you go into the settings on the side of the HUD, you can search for specific avatars," said Paige. "But that's going to have to wait until after we head back into the house."

"*Head back in there?*" I said. "Are you nuts?"

"Think about it, Rich," said Paige. "This is a *game*. You're a new player. The servenets put you in the standard house opening. Even though they only gave you a machete to start and me a shotgun with six—now three—shells, they're not that cruel. There should be a stash inside. We need to find it, otherwise we'll never make it far enough to meet Lars's friends."

"So your plan is to head back into the house that's infested with zombies, armed only with a blade and a shotgun with three shots left, and hope we don't get our faces torn off before we find some better guns?"

"It's the only smart thing to do," said Paige as she loaded the remaining shells into her gun's breech. "We already roused them. They should be massed at the bathroom door. Easy pickings."

I wiped a hand across my face. "I can't believe we're going to do this."

"Well, you'd better get used to it." Paige pumped the shotgun's action. "We're just getting started."

10

I snuck along the edge of the house, my feet making little more than a whisper in the soft, damp soil. Paige crept behind me, her shotgun at the ready.

I paused at the edge of the dilapidated dwelling and craned my neck around the side. A trio of drooping willows slouched lifelessly in the still of the night, moss trailing from their limbs down to the roots below. A flag hung from a pole stuck in the home's covered porch, its cloth layers folded over one another without any wind to fill its sails. Sweat beaded at my temples, more from the heat and humidity than my own exertion.

I gave Paige a nod and headed toward the terrace. I kept my eyes peeled, but nothing moved. Though I could've used a gust of wind to wipe the sweat from my brow, the stillness made my surveillance easier.

A floorboard creaked as I set foot upon it, and I paused, holding my breath. Paige swept the surroundings with her shotgun, but not even a cricket chirped.

Carefully, I shifted my bulk up the remaining two steps and to the front door.

I crouched outside it, eyeing the peeling paint and deep gouges that marred its heavy construction.

"It's manual," said Paige in a low voice. "You'll have to turn the handle."

"I know that."

I reached out, testing the knob, but the door didn't give.

"It's locked," I said.

"No, really?" Paige nodded toward the side at a window whose boarding had been torn free and discarded. "Try that."

I made my way there, careful not to step on the broken boards and rusted nails. A ragged hole in the window beckoned with all the charm of a harpy's embrace. I didn't catch any movement from within, nor did I smell anything foul wafting my way, but I didn't drop my guard as I climbed in.

Glass crunched underfoot as I stepped into a study lined with bookshelves, the contents musty and old. A heavy, wooden desk provided the only hiding spot for a zombie, but with its face to me and a glimmer of diffuse moonlight at my back, I deemed its underbelly safe.

Paige joined me, and together we crept to the room's lone door. Paige reached for the handle. I stopped her with a hand to her forearm.

"What is it?" she said.

"This game is known for its realism, right?" I said. "You know, other than your standard inventory, medicine, and food and beverage related tropes, correct?"

Paige nodded. "Where are you going with this?"

"It's hot. Humid. Old house. Creaky wooden steps." I pointed at the door's hinges.

Paige smiled. "And here I thought you wouldn't even know what those were."

"I may not be able to operate a coffee machine on my own, but I'm familiar with how pre-actuator driven doors work."

"And you happen to have some lubricant on hand?"

"Perhaps," I said. "It all depends on how good this simulation is."

I switched my machete to my left hand and raked my hand through my hair, my fingers meeting resistance from the pomade. I worked my fingertips against the substance. When I pulled them back, I tested them against one another. They stuck.

Paige smiled again. "Don't ever let anyone tell you you're a dolt, okay?"

"Remind yourself," I said. "You're usually the instigator."

I smeared the pomade over the door's three hinges, hoping the greasy substance would do its job, then wiped the remainder on my pants before securing my blade back in my dominant hand. Paige hefted her gun and gave me another nod.

I pulled.

Silence. It was golden.

Paige took point, heading up the entranceway and over to the living room we'd so recently escaped. The lamp still shone weakly, illuminating a mob of zombies at the top of the staircase, all of them amassed around the bathroom door. Paige held up a fist, then pointed two fingers at the mob. I wasn't sure what that meant, but I kept my mouth shut, gripped my machete tight, and followed her close.

Up the stairs we went. One step. Two.

The zombies moaned and pounded on the bathroom door.

Three steps. Five.

More moaning. The zombie stench thickened.

Three quarters of the way up the stairs. A zombie turned.

Blast. Pump. *Blast.*

A dozen walkers crumpled to the floor, their bodies torn to shreds by buckshot. A couple tumbled down the stairs, while others flopped to the ground like dying fish. Not a one remained.

"Huh," I said as I loosened my grip on my machete and brought my arm down. "That was surprisingly easAAHH!"

A zombie lunged at me from out of a bedroom, latching onto my flak jacket with superhuman strength. I brought my hands up for protection, pushing the zombie's snarling face away with my left while driving the machete into its midsection, but not before the creature's momentum sent us toppling down the stairs.

The zombie's snarling muzzle hovered in front of my face as the room swirled around me. An inhuman scream assaulted my ears. Hot breath attacked my face while I bounced off the steps. Pain blossomed in my side and arms, and I feared the crunching might be from my own bones rather than the wooden planks underneath.

We slammed into the 'L' near the bottom of the stairs, causing the zombie to lose his grip and me to lose my machete. He rolled and slammed into the couch while I lingered several steps from the bottom.

My head swirled. My body ached. The zombie moaned and clawed at the ground, trying to orient itself. Paige followed down the stairs.

"Shoot it!" I said.

"Not yet," said Paige. "I'm down to my last shell."

"And our last zombie."

"Not quite."

A trio of moans erupted from around the room. Another walking corpse appeared from the entrance hall. A second surfaced from behind one of the couches. A third turned the corner from a door near the back.

"Oh, you've got to be kidding me," I said.

The zombie who'd joined me on the staircoaster rose and dove at me. I punched him in the face, grabbed my machete, and ripped it free from his chest before sending my boot crashing down onto his diseased melon. It crunched. Bits oozed out, and I gagged.

The nearest of the new zombies rushed the stairs, screaming and clawing at the air.

"Hold it off," said Paige, holding firm.

"What?"

"Just do it!"

I retreated toward Paige's position, kicking the thing as it neared me. The couch zombie bum rushed the first, creating a four-armed flailing mass of crazed rage.

"Pull the trigger," I said.

"Not yet!"

I slashed with my machete, shearing bits of flesh off the arms. I retreated into Paige's legs. The third zombie stumbled into the others at the base of the staircase.

A crack ripped through the air, turning the zombie's brains into a piece of flesh-toned wall art.

I turned, the smell of burnt powder thick in my nostrils. "Nice shooting, Pai—"

I chucked my machete at Paige's head while simultaneously pulling her tight against me, missing her but impaling the zombie who'd crept up behind her right between the eyes. The thing let out a wheezy groan and toppled, bouncing off the steps a few times before joining its pals at the bottom.

Paige gulped. "Uh...thanks."

"No problem."

She pressed up against me, her arm around my shoulders and the entire right side of her body pushed into my midsection. My flak jacket acted as a shield between the supple flesh of her breasts and my torso, but no such barrier existed between her curvy lower half and my man bits.

Paige gave me a raised eyebrow. "Rich...there's something hard poking me in the rear."

"I think that's your shotgun." I shifted, trying to dislodge it from between us.

Paige smiled. "You, uh...sure about that?"

"Yeah...this is getting uncomfortable. You're already inside my head. I'm not sure we need to ratchet the relationship up any further."

"Fair enough." Paige pushed herself off me, steadying herself on the step above. "But don't say I never try to cheer you up."

"Seriously? Awkward," I said. "Now let's search this place before any more walkers show up. You've proven yourself adept with that shotgun. I'd rather you keep it loaded."

Paige smiled again. "Was that a thinly veiled allusion?"

"Seeing as you're the one with the gun, no," I said. "Come on. Let's move."

11

I knelt on the edge of a hotel rooftop, bits of crumbled concrete crunching under my boots as I cast my gaze at the ruined cityscape below. The clouds had parted over the last hour, liberating the world's large moon to bathe the lands below in a mellow, bluish white glow. The temperature had cooled somewhat, but not enough to keep my brow dry or my heart from beating heavy from exertion. Somewhere in the distance, a siren wailed, and a rhythmic thumping of rotors hinted at a hulking metal bird nearby.

I tapped the side of my head twice to bring my HUD up. I checked the map, looking for the markers we'd set in place to indicate the position of Lars's former party. The map moved over my vision as I twisted my head.

I stopped when the markers aligned with a building down the street, about a block away—a retail store of some kind, perhaps a grocery or hardware supplier. I pointed it out.

"That's the place?"

"Gillian's Superfoods Plus. Appears to be." Paige stood next to me, nodding. She'd traded her pump action shotgun for a leaner, meaner black combat version with a folding stock and an eight shell magazine. An armored dirt bike jacket now covered her black tank top, and she'd strapped a katana with an enameled steel sheath to the back of the ensemble.

She wasn't the only one who'd upgraded. I'd moved my machete to my belt loop to make room for a Marks and Sons semi-automatic pulse rifle with an extended barrel and a high-density ninety kilowatt hour battery. The sucker could make zombies dance like methamphetamine-fueled Extros at a rave, but I'd already drained the battery to less than a third of its original capacity without finding a suitable replacement.

Luckily, I didn't need it thanks to the baby I now held in my arms. A fully loaded, fully automatic modular assault rifle, equipped with a reflex sight, visible laser, extended magazine, spotlight, and grenade launcher—but that wasn't all. Some crazy as nails modder had bolted a spinning buzz saw to the end of the muzzle, activated via a secondary trigger set to the side of the main firing mechanism. The whole thing hung loosely around my neck thanks to a skull and crossbones guitar strap someone had jury-rigged for the task.

Paige looked across the expanse between us and the shop. "Doesn't look too bad. Street seems clear. I say we move in quick, making as little noise as possible, and hopefully we'll avoid any confrontations that could draw attention."

"Sounds good," I said. "Want me to lead?"

"With that new toy of yours? I definitely don't want you behind me."

I smiled. Though I'd taken my time warming up to the game, the addition of Buzzy McFaceripper to my arsenal had definitely upped the enjoyment factor.

I stood and shifted the rifle to my side, letting it hang fully from the black guitar strap that reeked of stale beer and death metal. I hooked my feet over the edge of a safety ladder, lowering myself rung by rung in the caged portion at the top before eventually reaching the open section below, at which point I slid down it with my hands and feet at the sides, skidding down in bursts to avoid rope burn on my hands.

I hit the ground and immediately transitioned into a light jog, my feet skipping over the cracked pavement below which glistened under the combined efforts of the moonlight and a sheen of dew. I heard a light thump of feet behind me and checked to make sure Paige followed before continuing at a brisk pace down the street. I stuck to the middle, in plain sight should anyone be watching but far from any potential lurkers or cars equipped with hair-trigger alarms—which they all were. Apparently every car in the game had seen its security system serviced by an auto technician with a vendetta against carjackers and a severe case of Parkinson's disease. *Realism, my ass.*

I closed on the front door of the greengrocer, pausing as I waited for Paige to catch up. When she did, I wasted no time, swinging open the front door and stepping into the breach, activating the light on my assault rifle as I did so. The glare might attract zombies, but lacking a non-infrared set of night vision goggles, it was my best bet.

I swept the beam back and forth as I waded towards aisles laid bare by the grime-caked hands of scavengers. Tin cans stripped of their labels littered the floor, some covered in a long since evaporated slime, others wallowing in seas of corn dust, cereal ground to powder by the mindless shuffling of undead feet.

I heard a howl and pivoted. A zombie lurched at me from underneath a checkout counter. I pulled on my trigger, sending high speed lead tearing through its corpse.

Two more howls. I spun left and right, firing hot death into the skulls of shamblers, my rifle thumping into my shoulder with every round fired. Paige's shotgun ripped through the air. *Blast.* Pump. *Blast.* Pump. *Blast.*

"There's a safe house in the back, I think," she called. "Let's move!"

I spurned my legs into gear, flying down one of the aisles with Buzzy at the ready. Rotting faces reared up out of the darkness, flashing me their rotting yellow teeth and bloodshot eyes. My rifle sang, the whip crack of the gunshots taking first billing to the steady melodic tinkle of the shells bouncing off the tile. My muzzle glowed from the steady discharge, hot and vicious.

The safe house door materialized in front of me. I rushed it, but an enormous corpse moved to block me— over two meters tall and at least a hundred and fifty kilos. I swapped my trigger finger to the side, sending the saw whizzing into action. I lunged and howled, swinging the spinning blade in a wide arc. Spin. Slice. Jab. The enormous herker disappeared in a cloud of blood and entrails.

The safe house door imploded under the force of my boot heel. Gristle and ichor dripped from my face as I dashed into the room. I cut loose with a primal scream, holding up my weapon to the skies and feeling a surge of adrenaline flow through my veins with a burst of masculine, virile power.

A quintet of individuals sat on an L-shaped couch, staring at me, nonplussed. The one on the end, with shaggy hair and an air of disinterest, took a sip of his beer and flicked a finger at me. "Who the hell is this douchenozzle?"

Paige hopped through the door after me, smashing it shut, locking the deadbolt, and sliding a wooden slat into place behind it for security.

I shifted from my action hero pose to a more traditional stance. "This douchenozzle has a name. Rich Weed, and I'll let you know I just sliced and diced my way through hordes of slobbering zombies to get here. So show a little respect."

The wannabe punk rocker brushed the hair out of his eyes and took another sip of his beer. "Uh...*yeah.* On easy."

"*Easy?*" I glanced at Paige.

She shrugged and gave me a reluctant smile. "Well, what did you expect? That I'd set it to expert right off the bat? The only games you play on a regular basis are tile-matching and repetitive tapping sorts of things."

My stance drooped into more of a slouch. "Oh."

The emo dude gave me an idle wave with his beer hand. "Seriously, bro, we're not interested. We've already got a party, and we're way out of your league."

"No," I said, lowering my rifle to let it hang from the strap. "That's not why I'm here. We're looking for someone. Two someones, actually. Paige?"

"PinkOniGirl and DreadMysterio59," said Paige. "That you?"

A girl in the back with a metallic purple bob that swept across her forehead lifted a hand. "I'm Oni. That's Dread." She pointed to the side of the couch, where a muscular dark-skinned man with an oriental dragon shaved into his millimeter-length hair sat. "What do you want?"

I thanked my lucky stars Dread wasn't the guy with the beer. "We're here to ask you about Lars."

"Who?" said Oni.

"XXEliteForce420XX."

"Oh, right. Leetforce," said Oni. "He signed off a few hours ago. What of him? You, uh...joining him in a party?"

I glanced at Paige. "A few hours ago? You're sure?"

Dread and Oni shared a similar glance as the one Paige and I had. Dread narrowed an eye. "Look, man. Richweed or whatever handle you go by. We're Leet's friends, but we don't hang out with him *all* the time. Whatever you had going on, that's between the two of you."

"I'm not here about a missed connection," I said. "Look, I don't know how to break this to you, but...Lars? Leetforce? He's dead."

"What are you talking about?" said Dread. "We ventured into a few high level areas and had some close calls, but nobody died. Besides, are you dense? We already told you he logged out."

"I don't mean in game," I said. "In real life. He's dead."

Dread snorted and waved a hand at me. "Get out of here, man."

"Told you," said the punkrock dude. "Douchenozzle."

"No, seriously," I said. "I didn't come here to meet Lars, or Leetforce. I'm not a gamer—"

"Obviously..." muttered one of the other couch crew.

"—I'm a private investigator. Leet's mother—real mother—hired me to track him down, to try to reconnect with him after spending several decades apart out of fear of personal interaction. We tracked Lars to his apartment but couldn't contact him, either physically or via Brain missive, so we set up some surveillance systems and eventually found that Lars was, well...*dead*. He passed away weeks ago if the state of his body is any indication."

"His mother wanted to reconnect?" said Oni. "That's really sweet. My parents have never shown the slightest interest in me. I mean—ZOMBIE!"

Oni pulled a handgun and unloaded two rounds, one after the other, through a window at the side of the room. Cracks radiated out from the bullet holes in the glass, the pair so close together to be virtually indistinguishable. On the other side, the zombie who'd stood there groaned and slid down the pane, leaving a bloody handprint on the glass.

"And that's how it's done, noob," said the emo dude, taking another sip of his beer.

"Hey, I may use more ammo, but I get the job done," I said. "Besides, it's not as if your girl over there couldn't have done better. She wasted a bullet when one would've sufficed."

"It's called a double tap," said Oni. "Learn it. But that walker got us off topic. What I was going to say was, regardless of his family situation, there's no way Leetforce is dead, especially if the person you found croaked weeks ago. He was playing with us a few *hours* ago."

"Seconded," said Dread. "You're barking up the wrong tree."

I glanced at Paige.

She shrugged. "Their stories match Princess's servenet logs."

"What about Leet's behavior?" I asked Oni. "Had he...changed at all? Behaviorally, I mean. Within the last few weeks."

"No," said Oni. "Look, this must be some sort of mistaken identity situation. I'm telling you, Leet's fine, physically and mentally."

"What about you?" I asked Dread. "What do you say?"

He snorted and rolled his eyes.

"Dude, you're clearly not going to believe us," said the beer-infused malcontent on the end. "So go ask his girlfriend, instead."

"Girlfriend?" I said. "Lars had a *girlfriend?*"

"*Leetforce has* a girlfriend," said Oni. "Seriously, what world do you live in?"

I understood now. She meant in game. "What's her avatar?"

"TriumphCat. She's—" Oni adopted that semi-glazed look indicative of someone accessing their Brain. "Oh. Never mind. She's playing Strike Force Zeta, and if I remember correctly, her clan is bombarding the Silurian base today. You'd get slaughtered out there. I'll send her a message. Tell her to meet you in the hub world if she gets a chance. But you have to promise me something first."

"What?" I said.

"Don't be creepy," said Oni. "You know, talking about Lars this and that. I mean, seriously, dude. Get a clue."

"I'll do my best," I said. "But only if you answer me one question first."

"Being?" said Oni.

"How do I get out of this game? I've kept my eyes peeled for glowing portals without seeing even a hint of one."

The couch crew stared at me with a bevy of raised eyebrows. Some of their jaws dropped. Paige slapped her forehead.

I gulped. "Did I, uh...mention I skipped the new gamer orientation?"

12

I sat on a park bench in the aptly named Princess City, the sprawling metropolis that served as Princess Gaming's most prestigious and luxurious hub city. Tall oak trees and maples, some reaching thirty meters into the sky, cast shadows over the lawn that stretched in front of me, while skyscrapers ten to fifty times as tall pierced the sky behind them. The trees failed to shade me, sitting as I was at the side of a running trail that circled a pond before dipping back into the trees, but I didn't mind. Unlike Cetie, the air was deliciously brisk. A breeze blew gently but consistently, enough to cool me to the touch but not enough to muss my hair or whip the edge of my guayabera into my face.

"I wonder if it ever rains here," I said.

Paige, sitting next to me on the bench, shrugged. Like me, she'd ditched her gear from Marked 4 Death, reverting to her monochrome tank top and garish leggings. "Probably not. If people want rain, they can get that in one of the innumerable sims and games available to them. The hubs are supposed to appeal to as many people as possible."

Off in the distance, flying cars whipped to and fro in the aisles between buildings creating multi-tiered stacks of traffic ten and twelve layers high. Tubes snaked between the tops of the skyscrapers, each of them shooting passengers through their innards like high speed nonaqueous waterslides, and levitating trains whisked back and forth along elevated rails, carrying gamers and NPCs alike to all stretches of the city.

All the varied methods of transportation were completely inefficient, of course. They weren't science fiction, but no sane civil engineer would ever design such a system in real life. The power expenditures for flying cars were absurd, levitating trains had been phased out in favor of sealed high speed vacuum pods ages ago, and personal transport tubes, as fun as they seemed, were expensive, created logistical nightmares, and chafed terribly. Not to mention all the methods of transport were entirely superfluous given Princess's portal fast travel system—which, as if turned out, I could access from anywhere at any time. It was how Paige and I had moved from Marked 4 Death to the serene tranquility of the park.

I almost remarked that it would've been nice to be a Princess programmer, not having to worry about real world concerns like energy usage and urban planning when creating massive hub worlds, before I remembered that programming was never as fun as using the end product. Besides, it wasn't as if the programmers didn't have to adhere to certain rules and regulations, including the plastering of Princess Gaming promotional materials on virtually every surface. On the faces of skyscrapers, billboards, floating in mid-air via enormous holodisplays, even on the very bench we now sat were the various Princess slogans. 'We get gamers!' 'A haven for Intros!' And my favorite: 'At Princess, the only rule is—have fun!' Every single display popped brightly in bubblegum pink and showed Johnny Masters and his cheesy, plasticized smile. Some of them even had him firing his trademark finger guns.

A portal sliced through the air not ten meters from our bench, and out of it stepped a suit of power armor, a meter and sixty tall, lacquered blue and gleaming in the sunlight except where covered with thick, green viscera. The suit stepped toward me, surprisingly lightly given its size, and paused two meters out. The tinted hemisphere of the suit's helmet retracted with a puff, disappearing into the headrest at the back. From its shadow emerged a woman with tan skin, dark eyes, and long brown hair held back in a pony tail.

"Are you Richweed?" she asked.

"In the flesh," I said. "Or...not. You know what I mean. This is my Brain, Paige. You're TriumphCat?"

She nodded. "Call me Cat. You game with your Brain?"

Paige gave me a look. "Told you."

I shrugged it off. "I do. I'm a noob, and I'll own it—at least I will now that I've realized what difficulty level I was playing on in Marked 4 Death."

"I got Oni's message," said Cat. "What do you want? As you can see, I'm sort of in the middle of something, and my squad could use me."

Now that she'd closed to within an arm's length, I could see various *bits* within the green goop on her body armor. Entrails, antenna fragments, and pieces of exoskeleton—mandibles and carapaces that had been blown to smithereens.

"What exactly were you fighting?" I asked.

"Silurians," said Cat.

"Come again?"

Cat snorted and frowned. "Silurians. The insect overlords of Strike Force Zeta. Seriously, are you here to waste my time or what?"

"Sorry," I said. "I'll get right to it then. The name's Rich Weed, not Richweed. I'm a private investigator, and I'm afraid I have to share the news that your boyfriend, Leetforce? Well...there's no easy way to say it. He's dead."

Cat's brow furrowed. "I'm going to kill Oni. Look, pal, I get that you're new to gaming and all, but these are *sims*. Like, *not real life*. I'm not sure what Leet ran up against in Marked 4 Death or Asteroidmageddon or whatever he was playing with you, but I'm sure he's fine."

"Yes, I got several of those same withering glances from your friends already," I said. "I'm serious, though. We found him—the real him, Lars—in his Cetie apartment a few hours ago, frail and lifeless. I haven't seen the coroner's report yet, but I'd guess he passed away several weeks ago."

Cat glanced around, confused. "Is this a prank? You're showing up as a real person in my HUD, so I know you're not a gag NPC. Who put you up to this?"

"This isn't a joke," I said, standing. "Ask Paige. She'll back me up."

Cat didn't ask, but Paige nodded anyway, standing and joining me at my side.

"Okay, let's assume you are who you say," said Cat. "I don't know who you found dead in his apartment, but it wasn't Leet. I saw him this morning, right before I signed into Strike Force Zeta. He's fine."

"That's what your boyfriend's pals Oni and Dread said, too," I said. "But the apartment where we found the dead man, an apartment registered to Lars Busk in the public listings, contained a man who looked a lot like the directory photo of Lars Busk. The same Lars Busk who supposedly owns the XXEliteForce420XX handle."

"This is ridiculous," said Cat. "Leet was peachy this morning, and I'm sure he's still fine. Now if you'll excuse me, I have better things to do than argue with you. Namely, stomping bugs into piles of twitching goo."

Cat turned and took two steps toward the portal.

"So I take it Leet normally takes extended breaks like this during the day?" I said.

Cat paused and turned her head. "What?"

"I'm assuming you and Leet keep similar schedules," I said. "Sleep at the same time, game at the same time. He signed off, what? About four, five hours ago? What do you suppose he's up to? Taking a nap? Enjoying an extended lunch?"

Cat stared at me, her eyes thoughtful. "Could be."

"But he doesn't normally, does he?"

Cat took a moment to respond. "No. Not normally."

"Does he normally say goodbye to you before he signs off?" I asked.

"Yes."

"And did he this time?"

Cat shook her head.

"Give him a call," I said.

"What?" said Cat.

"You're his girlfriend," I said. "If you give him a Brain call, he'll answer it, won't he? Even though he's not in game, right?"

"Yeah, of course he would. Give me a sec."

Cat tilted her head to the side, and I waited. After about twenty seconds, she turned back to face me. "He's not answering."

I took a step forward. "I'm sorry."

"*What?* No," said Cat. "He's fine. I'm sure of it. You said this guy you found had been dead for weeks. I told you, I spoke to Leet this morning, and the morning before that, and the one before that. Whoever you found, it *wasn't Leet.*"

"Did you notice any change in his behavior?" I asked. "Specifically, around the time the man we found might've passed? Three, four weeks ago?"

Cat shook her head. "Nothing. Leet hasn't changed at all. He's the same Leet I've always known. He hasn't done anything out of the ordinary."

"Until today," I said.

Cat sighed. "Yes."

"Look, Cat," I said, donning my sensitivity cap. "I can only imagine what thoughts must be going through your mind right now, but know that I'm of the opinion you might be right. It's entirely possible the man we found wasn't Leet, but I need your help to figure out what's happening."

Cat chewed on her lip. "Okay. Fine. I'll help. What do you need?"

"Obviously, if he contacts you via Brain or if he logs back in and meets you in game, let me know," I said. "But beyond that, I need to sift through his life. See if anything is out of place. I tried to do that in his— Lars's—real life apartment without much success. Does he have a place of his own here in the Princess hub world?"

"Sort of," said Cat. "We share an apartment."

"Perfect," I said. "I don't suppose you could show me there?"

Cat gave me a single nod. "Sure. Give me a moment to pop back into Strike Force Zeta and let my squad know I'll be MIA for a while. Meet me at the lobby of four forty Haldeman Plaza in five minutes or so."

"Will do," I said.

Cat stepped back through the portal. It winked shut behind her. I stared through the spot at the grass and waving maple branches behind it.

"You okay, Rich?" asked Paige.

I blinked. "Yeah. I just really hope I'm wrong about Leet. I hate breaking this sort of news to people. It's why I chose private investigation over police work, you know."

"Really?" said Paige. "I thought you chose private investigation because the hours were better and because you didn't feel confident you'd pass the basic competence exam."

"Remind me again why I keep you?"

Paige smiled. "Because I'm charming and vivacious. And because you couldn't even figure out how to access the menu of a Brain game without me."

I snorted. "The truth comes out eventually. Come on. Let's get a move on."

13

My portal spit me out in front of a swanky high rise that soared into the sky, challenging the wispy clouds swirling above it with its sharp spire. Blossoming cherry trees lined the street outside, and gold trim edged the half-dozen tinted glass doors that faced the roadway. Despite their modern, automatic construction, a pair of doormen outfitted in sharp red coats and caps stood at attention on either side. I couldn't imagine a more tedious and unnecessary position, but I doubt the pair cared. My mini map indicated they were NPCs. The programmers had likely equipped them with little more than a few maps of the city and a minimal understanding of polite conversation.

I brought up my HUD and checked the settings. "What's wrong with this thing? I told it to warp us into the lobby."

"Oh, heavens, no," said Paige. "You mean you'll have to walk a whole fifty meters to get where you're going?

Good thing you're in tip top shape. All this virtual exercise would kill a lesser man."

"It's not that," I said. "What if I requested to travel to the edge of a canyon and the Princess servenets created for me a portal fifty meters beyond where I'd asked? Not so small of a problem anymore, am I right?"

"It's an intentional design," said Paige. "You forget this is a hub world. Its whole purpose is for people to interact, so the designers made it so you couldn't warp directly into or out of your virtual apartment. Yes, Intros are much more sociable in online settings, but habits are hard to break. By forcing people to walk into and out of their apartments every time, down the elevators and through the lobby, the developers encourage social interaction which is good for all parties. Besides, it's an homage to the very origins of gaming. Did you know early gamers were grouped together and placed into parties in places called lobbies? It was just text on a screen at that point, but still."

"Sounds thrilling."

I stepped forward, the doors parting for me, and entered the lobby. The ceiling stretched high overhead, with waves of thin, green fiber optic cables hanging down, each of them sparkling and shimmering intermittently like a rainforest shower. Burnished copper covered the walls, and the tile floor had been polished to a mirror shine. People milled about the insides, both real users and NPCs according to my HUD. No aliens, though.

That, I didn't find particularly surprising. Princess Gaming was a Cetie based operation, and the spaceport not withstanding, the planet wasn't the most diverse of places. I imagined if any aliens were present in the hub world, they'd probably congregate in buildings more suited to their physiologies, with higher ceilings and larger furniture for the Diraxi and the opposite for the Meertori—although at least in the virtual world, the latter could ditch their pressurized methane-based respirators. I was, however surprised to find so many non-Cetiean body types among those congregated in the lobby. Because of pervasive genetic engineering that blessed us all with chiseled features, I'd figured most users would keep their standard appearance in game, but the most popular body type appeared to be that of the taller, more slender Gaians, not us squat and compact Cetieans. I even spotted a few super tall, skinny types, modeled after spacers or Martians, I supposed.

"Hey! You ready?"

I jumped and turned. TriumphCat had snuck up behind me, which would've been quite a feat if she hadn't ditched her suit of glossy blue power armor along the way. As it was, she'd dropped a couple centimeters and about fifty kilos, revealing a svelte Gaian body type simply dressed in jeans and a sleeveless navy blouse.

"Hey," I said. "That was quick."

"I move fast," she said. "It's easy when you're not standing around gawking at everything."

"It's involuntary," I said. "I come from a long line of gawks."

"*Gawks?*" said Cat. "What the heck is that? A planet?"

"No, it's a little self-deprecating grammar joke," I said. "Never mind. You show the way. We'll tail you."

Cat nodded and headed toward the elevators. Paige and I followed. We took the lift up to the forty-fourth floor, where Cat led us down another copper coated hallway and through a set of wide doors that blinked open upon her approach.

I whistled as I walked in. The lobby hadn't unfairly boosted expectations for the rooms. The apartment put my luxury penthouse suite to shame. It had everything. Plush furniture. Thick carpets. Gleaming tile floors and high ceilings. A brilliant view, room to spare, and of course, not a single speck of dust or grime to be found—because why would those exist in a virtual world? Folks crazy enough to seek filth out could do so in Marked 4 Death, like I had.

"No wonder gamers spend all their waking hours in game," I said to Paige. "Look at this place."

"Questioning your commitment to the real world?" she said.

"Not quite," I said. "But I can see the appeal."

"So," said Cat. "We're here. I can show you around if you like, but I'm still not entirely sure what you're hoping to find."

"Neither am I," I said. "Why don't we start over here?"

"In the kitchen?" said Cat. "Sure. As you can see, it's a, uh...place to prepare food?"

I wandered over and starting pulling on drawers and performing a cursory examination of the utensils. "Mind if I ask you some questions about Leet?"

Cat stayed in the living room. "Sure, I guess."

"How did you guys meet?"

"In a party," she said. "You know how it is."

"Not really," I said. "As I made clear earlier, I don't really do this sort of thing. I'm more of a casual gamer. Smashblocks. That sort of thing."

Cat looked at me like I was crazy. "What's the appeal in that?"

I shrugged as I kept sifting. "I can do it between cases. I don't know. It's strangely addictive."

"Right," said Cat. "Well, anyway, Leet and I met playing...what was it? Rogue Nation: Black Ops, I think. We were in separate parties. Terrorist gunfire forced us together. A lot of our friends went down, but Leet and I managed to sneak through an air vent and shoot our way out. He was really quick on the draw, but it was more than his marksmanship and overall play I liked. Even with bullets raining down around us, he was goofy and fun. We just clicked. Started playing together more and more. Been together ever since."

I peeked in the refrigerator. "How long ago was that?"

"Four or five years, give or take," said Cat.

"Do people get married in game?" I asked.

"Say *what*?"

I closed the fridge and turned back to Cat, who stood there with a befuddled expression. "Sorry. Did I overstep a line?"

"No, it's...okay," said Cat, shaking her head and causing her brown hair to sway. "Some people do. We haven't. It's come up though. Recently."

"Like, three weeks ago recently?"

Cat's eyes hardened. "No."

"Just checking. Let's keep going."

Cat gave me the grand tour, showing me the dining room, home theater, various living quarters, and master suite, where Leet's possible death kept me from making a crass remark about the various Princess fantasy worlds not being the only place where magic happened. Upon first glance, I couldn't understand what struck me as odd about the master bathroom, which featured a huge walk-in shower and claw-footed soaker tub, but then I realized the omission: the toilet. No need for that in the virtual world, apparently.

"And finally, this is our study," said Cat as she led Paige and me into another room with a fabulous view. A pair of molded Pseudaglas desks sat side to side overlooking the cityscape, holoprojectors mounted above each one. I could almost imagine Leet and Cat sitting at the pair, side by side, each of them going through their messages, Cat checking on the status of her insect murder squad and Leet trashing all of my Brain missives.

"You have a *study?*" I said.

"It's another place to hang out," said Cat. "All the units have them. So...see? I told you. Nothing weird or out of place or suspicious anywhere in our apartment. It's our little slice of heaven, nothing more and nothing less."

I pointed to a wall. "What's in the cabinet?"

Cat glanced at it, a white rectangular boxy thing that reached to hip level. "Oh. Those are Leet's, um...love letters. To me."

"*Letters?*" I said. "Like paper and ink and words sort of letters?"

"Yes."

"Who does that nowadays?" I said. "It's hard enough to even find the components needed to make one."

"It's easy when you can digitize everything involved," said Cat. "And I guess Leet was old fashioned like that. I mean, *is* old fashioned. Damn..."

Cat sighed. I caught a flash of something on her cheek in the sunlight. She brought a thumb up to wipe it away.

I felt Paige's light touch on my arm. "Rich? Maybe it's time we go."

"What?" I lowered my voice to a whisper. "Are you kidding? Love letters? Those could be a potential gold mine, at least if he's kept writing them on a regular basis. We can track Leet's behavior. See if he's changed over time."

Paige shook her head. "Not now. Maybe later. Give her time."

Cat wiped her cheek again. As always, Paige was right, even if I didn't like the results.

"Cat?" I said. "Thanks for letting us in and showing us around. We're going to head out, but we'll update you if we discover anything else about Leet or the man we believe to be Lars. Hopefully you'll be willing to do the same?"

Cat nodded, but didn't turn. "Yeah. Sure."

"Can we communicate outside the game if need be?"

Another nod. "My name's Juanita Villafranca. I'll send you my contact. Brain calls only, though. I...don't do well with people."

I tried to think of something reassuring to tell her, some high point to leave on, but I couldn't. Given the circumstances, optimism seemed unfounded. Paige put her hand on my shoulder, and we headed for the door.

14

The elevator door opened with a ding as Paige and I approached it. We both stepped inside, I asked for the ground floor, and it lurched into motion. The interior of the elevator door gleamed, its copper coating polished to a sheen like every other surface in the swanky apartment complex. I saw my own face in the reflection, slightly muddled from the metal's refractive properties, but next to me, rather than Paige, I swear I caught a hint of Cat, her face drooping and a sparkle of tears on her cheek.

I blinked and shook my head. "I said it before, and I'll say it again. I really hope I'm wrong about Leet."

"It's one thing to deal with a criminal," said Paige. "It's another thing entirely to face the aftermath of a criminal's actions on someone's family or loved ones."

"I don't know how cops do it." I turned to face Paige. "Wait...a criminal? Are you saying you think someone killed Lars?"

"That actually wasn't what I was implying," said Paige, "but since you bring it up, I admit it's a possibility."

"Is that what you think happened?"

"I can't really speculate without having more information," said Paige. "Besides, it's not really part of our investigation. That's for the police to determine."

The elevator slowed and spit us out. I walked with Paige toward the front doors, chewing on my lip and staring at the floor the entire time.

"Something on your mind?" asked Paige.

I looked up. "You can't tell?"

"Yes and no. Clearly I can tell, but due to the specific architecture of the Princess Gaming servenets, your avatar and mine are separate. I can't actually control all the things I normally would. It's why I wasn't able to bring up your HUD remotely during Marked 4 Death. I had to actually tap your temple twice. I also can't read your thoughts. It's simultaneously refreshing and disconcerting."

I got the general gist of her discourse and gave in without protest. "Okay. So here's what I'm thinking. Maybe it's wishful thinking because I hate seeing damsels like Cat in distress, but the more I mull it over, the more convinced I am Leet isn't dead."

"*Leet.* But not Lars."

"Correct—sort of," I said. "The way I see it, between the timing of Lars's death and his apparent online presence until a few short hours ago, we're facing one of two possible outcomes. Either the man we found in Lars's apartment is indeed Lars Busk, and someone has stolen his identity and is posing as him online, or the man we found *isn't* Lars Busk, and the real Busk is safe and sound somewhere, continuing his gamer identity as LeetForce undeterred.

"If the first scenario is true, then we need to figure out why someone would want to take over Busk's identity, because the reasons for doing so aren't immediately obvious. What's there to gain from taking over the life of a reclusive Intro who, based on his surroundings, had little if any wealth and resources to his name?"

"To steal his online girlfriend?" offered Paige.

"I suppose that's possible," I said, "but if Cat and her friends are to believed, Leet hasn't changed his online behavior, well...*ever,* really—which is why I hold out some hope about her and Leet. It's possible she's never come across Lars's true online avatar. That the man she knows as Leet is an impostor, but the same impostor she's always known, if that makes any sense."

Paige nodded. "There might be some trust issues between the two of them, but at least Leet would be alive in that scenario."

"The other possibility is far more confusing," I said. "If the man we found in Busk's apartment isn't Lars, then that's great news for Cat. Leet may be alive and well and exactly who he claims to be. But then who did we find dead in Busk's gaming chair, and where is Lars? And more importantly, why swap places with someone else? Why the subterfuge?"

Paige shrugged as we exited through the front doors. "I'm not sure, but the identity of the dead man should be easy to ascertain—for the police, anyway. I'm not sure they'll be eager to share that information with you, though."

I flashed a smile. "Why wouldn't they? I'm such a nice guy."

Paige snorted. "Yeah, I'm going to cast another vote into the 'glad you didn't become a cop' pile. I don't think you would've lasted long with such a cavalier attitude."

"My distaste for rules and regulations notwithstanding, I think I would've made a great cop," I said. "You know, except for the other reasons we already discussed, like not being able to deal with grieving friends and family or the schedule."

"That's the other problem with me not lurking inside your head in game," said Paige. "I can't stop you from putting your foot in your mouth."

"Then we better move out as quickly as we can," I said. "Why don't you bring up one of those glowing portal thingies and get us out of here?"

Paige shook her head. "I'll refrain from harping on the orientation session again and simply say those are for in universe travel only. Check your HUD settings for a log out option."

I did as Paige suggested, found the button, and mashed it with a mental flick. The Princess cityscape faded, replaced instead with the inside of my living room. Gone was the gentle breeze that carried with it scents of the cherry blossoms, replaced instead by new sensations—a stiffness in my legs and back, as well as a notable pressure coming from the direction of my bladder.

Carl sat on the couch cushions where I'd left him. He looked at me as I glanced around, reorienting myself. "Ah, Rich. You're back. How was it?"

"Interesting, if not necessarily as enlightening as I'd hoped," I said. "How long was I in there?"

"Three hours, forty seven minutes, and change," said Carl. "Why?"

"Just making sure I don't have any urological problems in need of being addressed. I'll tell you about it in a moment."

I stood and headed to the bathroom. As I started to relieve myself, I heard a familiar voice in the back of my mind.

Ah. This does feel nice, doesn't it?

I almost stopped in mid-stream. *Excuse me? Since when do you get off on my bodily functions.*

What? said Paige. *I was talking about being back in your Brain where I belong. Get your mind out of the gutter.*

Yeah, like I'm supposed to believe your impeccable timing was an accident.

Paige snickered but didn't respond. Of course, that was response enough.

I zipped up and headed back to the living room, where I briefed Carl on what we'd learned from Oni, Dread, and Cat, as well as regaled him with tales of my brave exploits in Marked 4 Death, which I could tell from his vacant expression he found all-consuming. He perked up when I shared my theories about the possible connections or lack thereof between Lars and Leet.

"So," said Carl with a perfectly raised eyebrow, "you really think the man we found in Lars's apartment, who resembled the photo of Lars we had on file, isn't actually Lars?"

"I'm not saying I believe it," I said, "but it's an avenue we owe it to ourselves to investigate. If nothing else, it's an avenue the police will chase. Speaking of which...Paige? Can we give that officer from the crime scene a call? Sanz, was it?"

Time to test your sweet talking skills?

"Don't you know it."

I heard the trill of a Brain call. A few moments later the center of my vision blurred and a person appeared. Officer Sanz, seated in an uncomfortable looking chair in front of a flat gray cubicle backdrop. I didn't realize Sanz would answer my call with a visual feed, but then again, police officers were trained in the physiological aspects of lie detection, so I could see why he'd want to meet me face to face.

He smiled, looking far more cheerful than anyone in his position and stuck in such a bland environment had a right to be. "We meet again, Mr....Weed, correct?"

"That's right," I said. "How are you doing, Officer Sanz?"

"Well, I'm neck deep in about four different investigations," he said. "So I've been better. I'm glad to see you've changed your mind, though."

"Changed my mind? What are you talking about?"

"You know," said Sanz. "About you coming clean regarding your involvement in the Busk case. I'd be happy to take your revised statement if you're ready."

I blinked and stared into the projection. I'd completely forgotten about that particular conversation point.

"That *is* why you called me, isn't it?" said Sanz.

"The statement," I said. "Right. Well, to be honest, I had other things on my mind..."

Sanz rolled his eyes. "Come on, Mr. Weed. Really? Are we going to go through this again? I need to provide my superior officer with a clear, concise set of events leading up to Busk's death and the discovery of his remains, and your statement remains a lingering thorn in my side. Obviously you want something from me. Do you expect to get it without scratching my back first?"

I took a deep breath and forced it out through my nose. "Alright. Fine. I'll play ball."

"I'm listening."

"I snuck a micro surveillance bot into Busk's apartment through his exterior food delivery slot. That's how I knew he was dead."

I left out the part about me duping a lowly Smotrycz's service bot along the way. No need for me to come across as a liar *and* a sleazeball.

"See, Mr. Weed," said Sanz. "Was that so hard?"

"You're not going to press charges, are you?" I said.

"Why would *I* press charges?" he said. "That would be Lars Busk's choice to make, and he's dead. His next of kin might, but if the rest of your story is true, then you're already in his mother's employ with her blessing to do precisely as you did."

"Thanks."

"I'm a cop, not a steel girder," he said. "I can yield. Now let's get to business. What do you want?"

"Have you performed a DNA test on Lars's remains yet?"

"Perhaps," said Sanz. "Why do you want to know?"

I gave him the same spiel I'd given Carl and, before him, Paige. I was starting to feel like a bot stuck in an infinite feedback loop.

"So," I finished. "If I'm right about Leet's online presence, it's possible Lars is alive—somewhere."

Sanz sucked on his teeth. "Well, I have to say those are very interesting theories. They'll give us food for thought at the department."

"And the results of the DNA test?"

Sanz stared in response.

"Oh, come on," I said. "I updated my statement. I'm being a hundred percent honest now. And it's not as if I'm trying to get in the middle of your investigation. I just want a simple answer. I'm still in Miss Busk's employ, remember? What am I supposed to tell her? That I'm not sure, but her son may or may not be dead?"

Sanz shook his head. "Look. I get where you're coming from, but my hands are tied. All I can tell you is we're treating this as a criminal investigation for the time being. Once the autopsy is complete and we've finished the tests we want to run, I'll see what I can pass along. Hopefully, we won't find any evidence of foul play and I won't get a muzzle order thrown my way. Trust me, that would be the simplest outcome for both of us."

"So you'll let me know?" I said.

"I'll try."

I sighed. "Thanks. I guess that's all I can ask."

"Not a problem. I appreciate you coming clean. Sanz out."

The image of the police station interior blinked away, replaced once more by my own living room.

Carl gave me a nod, having followed along with the conversation thanks to Paige's efforts. "Well, that could've gone better. But knowing you, I'd say you could've fared far worse."

"I can't tell if that's a compliment or not," I said.

"How do you want to play this?" he asked.

"Well, I'm not going to give up, if that's what you're implying. I'd welcome Sanz's report, but who knows how long the police investigation is going to take. In the meantime, we can keep sleuthing, same as we always do. Chances are the police cleaned out Busk's apartment, but I doubt they had a professional crew come in. Nor did the Meertori building manager, if I know his type. I'll bet if we drop by tomorrow and slip another *donation* in front of the manager's respirator, he'd let us take a second look around Busk's apartment. Shouldn't be too hard to find a rogue hair somewhere that we could use for our own DNA analysis."

"And if the DNA comes back a match to Lars's servenet entry?"

"Let's take this one step at a time." I stood and cracked my neck. "First things first, I'm going to snag something to eat and get a proper night's rest. I know I didn't actually do anything, but Marked 4 Death really took it out of me."

"Rich?"

"Yes, Carl?"

My old pal gave me a concerned look. "We need to tell Miss Busk about what happened. I could understand waiting at first, but...she has a right to know."

I sighed. "I know. You're right. But let's give it one more day, at least until I've tried to recover DNA from

Lars's apartment. If I'm going to deliver heart-breakingly bad news, I at least want to make sure I'm right."

Carl nodded, and I headed toward the kitchen. Of course, Helena wasn't the only one I'd have to notify. There was Cat, too. I really didn't want to have to find out whose response would be worse.

15

I crept forward along a darkened hallway, my trusty buzz saw assault rifle amalgamation clenched between my hands. The floorboards creaked underneath me, and the walls to my sides stretched and loomed, pushing on my field of vision. The air floated around me like syrup, thick and hot and heavy. Sweat poured down my face and across my bare arms, slicking my palms and making my gun slip dangerously in my grasp.

I heard a howl off in the distance, like a wolf's but sadder, more piercing, and more human. I spun, poking the muzzle of my gun into the darkness. I flicked the light atop it with my thumb to no avail. The battery had died, and it wasn't coming back.

Where was Paige? She'd been here a moment ago, slinking behind me in the hallway's tight embrace. I could still hear her snide, jocular remarks and biting commentary about my personal life as if she were an arm's length at my back, yet when I turned I saw nothing. A hallway. No doors. No exits. Just darkness and walls, creeping ever closer. How long had I been down here? Where had the zombies gone? Their absence was something to cheer, wasn't it?

I heard the howl again and spun back in my original direction. The high-pitched baying had been closer this time and less wolf-like. A stench of fear filled my nostrils, blood and rot and human waste all mixed together in a noxious cocktail. I tried to grasp my rifle tighter, but my sweat worked against me.

Something wrapped a limb around me, and I screamed. I turned and wrenched on my trigger. Bullets flew, but not where I wanted them to. A creature, over two meters tall, covered in slime and scales and with an abundance of tentacles, slapped the rifle from my slippery fingers, sending it clattering to the ground. Several more tentacles shot forth, gripping my arms and legs and pinning me against the wall. Its gelatinous face split in two, displaying rows of razor-sharp teeth. Hot, rotting fish breath blew across my face, and the creature cut loose with a melodious, chime-like yell.

I paused in my struggle against the tentacles. Though my blood pumped furiously through my veins, my fear lessened. That hadn't been the haunting howl I'd expected.

The creature sucked air back through its mouth and let it out in another soft, ear-pleasing jingle.

Yup. Definitely not that scary.

I cracked an eye. Gone was the terrifying visage of an undead monster dredged from the deepest, blackest pits of the ocean, replaced instead with my nightstand, bedside lamp, and integrated holoclock. Everything was a dark shade of gray thanks to the automatic tinting on my bedroom windows.

Paige?

Morning, sunshine, she said.

I glanced at the clock and tried to process the numbers. It took me a little longer than it should've. *Why am I awake? I barely hit the hay four hours ago.*

Somewhere in the distance, I heard the creature from the black lagoon's throaty, melodious death jingle. It sounded suspiciously like my door chimes.

There's your answer, said Paige.

I groaned. *Why is it people always come by when I'm sleeping?*

Because God hates you?

You know I'm not religious, I said.

Sorry. Because a secular, deterministic universe hates you?

I tried to turn but found myself tightly bound in sheets. That explained the tentacles and the sweatiness. *Why hasn't Carl taken care of it? Whoever's there, I don't want any.*

He went out to buy groceries, said Paige. *You were running low on fruit, cheese, and buttermilk.*

Because I'm such a big buttermilk guy...

You ingrate. He was going to make you biscuits when you woke up.

The chimes sounded again, and I sighed. I wriggled and twisted, eventually liberating myself from the sheets' loose prison. Crossing over to my closet, I threw on the nearest pair of slacks and a breezy shirt. Before leaving my room, I glanced in the mirror. My feet were bare and my hair had become a home for wayward birds, but making a good impression on my caller was the last thing on my mind.

I headed out and started down the stairs.

By the way, you had several Brain calls while you were asleep, said Paige.

Any messages?

Nope.

So who called? I asked.

Not sure, said Paige. *It was an unlisted number.*

That was ominous. Few people had the clout or the wherewithal to get those.

I reached my front door, but I'd learned my lesson from prior experience. Instead of opening it blindly, I depressed a button on its side. In response to my touch, the door faded away, revealing the person on the other side, but only to me. Unidirectional transparency was a wonderful thing.

Just outside my apartment stood a man with a wide nose, creases around his mouth and forehead, and a two day old beard—probably not a Cetiean based on appearances. He stood a little too tall, his frame wasn't quite wide enough, and his dress was all wrong. A heavy gray suit jacket hung over his shoulders, and though his tie had been loosened and the top two buttons of his collar unbuttoned, the simple fact of his tie's existence spoke to his ignorance. A trilby hat with a black band around it perched on his head, tufts of thick, black hair poking out from underneath.

The man had his arms crossed and tapped his foot against the ground impatiently. His jaw muscles clenched and unclenched regularly, either from chewing gum or from a nervous tic.

Nothing about the guy made me feel warm and fuzzy or overly eager to meet him, which is why I was so surprised with myself when I instructed Paige to open the door anyway.

The entrance to my apartment blinked open. The guy looked up, a dull gleam in his eyes. "Rich Weed?"

"That's me," I said. "You are...?"

"Dirk Kriggler, PI," he said. "We need to talk."

Without another word, the man pushed past me into my apartment, making a bee line for my living room. The move caught me so off guard I didn't have time to react with a roundhouse kick to his head. Then again, the man hadn't attacked me outright. It would be imprudent to respond to his intrusion with violence, but a response of *some* form was necessary. I just wasn't sure of what kind.

16

I followed the guy into my home, joining him by the couches. He hadn't taken a seat, choosing instead to mill about with his arms still crossed, peering at my decorations and wall art and casting his gaze down hallways.

"You said your name was Kriggler?"

The man glanced at me and nodded. "That's right. Dirk Kriggler. PI."

"And I'm assuming that stands for private investigator?"

He gave me a sidelong look. "What else would it stand for?"

"I've been burned on the acronym before." Then, to Paige: *Mind looking that up for me? I thought I was the only private detective on Cetie.*

So did I, she said. *Give me a second.*

"So, *Dirk,*" I continued. "What brings you here?"

"A case." He shot a finger at me and leveled me with a sharp eye. "A big case. *Big.*"

"And you're investigating it," I said. "Because you're a private eye."

He ignored my sarcasm and began to pace back and forth across the living room. "Three weeks ago, a woman by the name of Sanika Gupta approached me in my office. Lovely woman. Talkative. Intelligent. Attractive. She presented to me what seemed like a simple case. Her husband, one Hari Gupta, who she'd long since divorced for his growing sloth and interpersonal problems, had stopped making payments for child and spousal support.

"Now Miss Gupta to me seemed quite capable, and in fact, she presented herself as a lawyer. I imagine her earnings were such that she had no real need of her husband's contributions, but if I'm being honest, I detected a hint of animosity in her toward him. Can't blame her. But I'm getting off track. The point is, after their divorce, Sanika obtained a court order to have Hari's government work stipend garnished for the support payments, just in case he refused to get a job, which she claimed was likely. The payments had come in, regular as afternoon rain, until recently, when they'd disappeared entirely."

"*Regular as afternoon rain?*" I said.

"They're regular where I come from," said Dirk. "Not like this sweltering hellhole."

"And where are you from exactly?" I asked.

"Lots of rain, lots of Guptas," said Dirk. "Come on. I thought you were a private eye."

I figured it out with the help of his nudge. Cetif, the other large inhabited planet in the Tau Ceti system. First settled by religious refugees of the Hindu variety, which explained the preponderance of last names of Earthen Indian origin. Unlike Cetie, which had required substantial terraforming to cool its surface to habitable levels, Cetif had required quite the opposite. The planet circled Tau Ceti at the outer edge of the star's habitable zone, and its atmosphere had needed quite a buildup of greenhouse gasses to bring its surface temperature to something acceptable for skin. Now, thick clouds shrouded the planet day and night, making it a damp, chill, dreary place only barely fit for the living—literally. Plants struggled to grow there due to the low insolation.

I couldn't imagine residing there, but I suppose I should've been grateful for the planet's presence. Without Cetif, Cetie never would've been populated. I wasn't an expert on terraforming, but apparently it was much easier to heat a planet up than cool it down. Twentieth century cultures figured that out the hard way.

Dirk snapped his fingers at me. "You still with me, pal?"

"More or less," I said. "I'm still trying to figure out why you're here, though."

"Because of Hari, of course," said Dirk, still pacing. "You see, I figured he wouldn't be too hard to track down. But Sanika? She thought otherwise. She already contacted Cetif's Department of Social Services to ask about the garnished stipend payments. They gave her the rigmarole, eventually referring her to their own internal fraud department that told her they couldn't send her portion of the payments until they confirmed Hari's physical location, seeing as his residence permit had lapsed.

"That's where I came in, of course. I tracked Hari down, or at least I tried. Wasn't too hard, but when I arrived at his place, after a bit of digging, I discovered he wasn't there. So I talked to some people. Turned some screws. Put some feet to the fire. Long story short, I learned Hari had emigrated. Can't blame him, really. I can see how he'd be upset, having to share his stipend payment with a disgruntled ex-wife with a well paying job, never mind how pleasant she seemed to me. So he skipped town. Skipped the whole planet, coming here instead."

"And you followed him," I said.

"Darn right I did," said Dirk.

For what it's worth, said Paige, *I think this guy might be telling the truth. I found evidence of a Kriggler Investigations in the most recent servenet stream from Cetif, and I also found that—shockingly—you're not the only private investigator on Cetie any more. A Dirk Kriggler applied for and received a private investigator's license two days ago.*

Guess I don't have a monopoly anymore, I said. "This still doesn't explain why you're here though."

"Of course it does," said Kriggler. "I have an obligation to my client to track down Hari. To make him pay up. If I couldn't do it through the garnishing of his Cetif government stipend, then I was sure as heck going to try to do the same with his Cetie work subsidy. So I came here to Cetie to do just that.

"Problem was, my Cetif PI license didn't do me a whole lot of good here. Had to apply for and gain a new one, and even once I had that, my options were limited. Oh, I was able to track Hari down, of course. Looked him up in the public listings, but when he refused to answer my calls, physical or digital, I didn't have many options. Whatever rights I had in Cetif due to Sanika's court order didn't transfer across planets, you understand.

"But I didn't let that stop me. Although Hari and Sanika's legal status didn't give me any real legal authority, it did provide me with a moral one. So I went on the warpath. Found Hari's bank, the one who'd been accepting his Cetie work stipend payments since he arrived. I talked to a sweet lady there, real sweet, and gave her the sob story. Divorced mother of four, on the ropes. A deadbeat dad who'd do anything to get away, even skip the planet. She bought right in. Though she couldn't help me with my wage garnishing situation, she was able to, or at the very least *willing* to, provide me with a copy of Hari's bank records.

"And that's when things got interesting, because as it turns out, much to my chagrin, Hari's account was empty. Worse than empty. In the red. He had past due payments for rent, food, and a gaming subscription. You'd think his work stipend check would cover it, but that was being rerouted. Subtracted from his account before it even got there. Even if I had the legal authority to do so, there was nothing left to garnish. The whole thing reeked of corruption and malfeasance, so of course I couldn't leave it alone. I had to keep digging."

I held up a hand. "Look. Kriggler. I've tried to be patient and understanding, letting you into my apartment after being woken up half-way through my sleep cycle. And this is all very interesting, or at least it could be to someone who cared. But despite asking you over and over again, you still haven't told me why you're here.

Not on Cetie. Not in my suburb of Pylon Alpha. Right here, in my apartment, in my living room. Seriously. *Why are you here?"*

Kriggler stopped pacing and stared at me. "Isn't it obvious? I'm here because Hari is dead."

17

I blinked slowly. Perhaps I still hadn't fully woken up. Either that or I was still dreaming and it would only be a matter of time before Kriggler transformed into a hideous, multi-tentacled beast with a thoroughly unintimidating door chime scream. "Come again?"

"The cops were a little stunned when I called them," said Dirk. "To be fair, I was too when I found him. Emaciated. Disheveled. And the smell? Well, I don't want to bring it back to mind. And it wasn't just him. It was all that food on his counters and floor, spoiled beyond belief."

My ears perked. "So he'd been dead for a while, then?"

"At least three weeks, I'd say," said Kriggler. "Could be more. I'm no coroner, but there appeared to be about a month's worth of pizza on his counter, so take that how you will. Anyway, when the police arrived they questioned me thoroughly, seeing as I'd been the one to call it in. They were pretty tight lipped about everything, but I could tell something was off, and I'm not talking about the smell. More like they'd seen something similar and not that long ago. I overheard one of them mention another private eye, and then they dropped your name. Weed. I asked about you, of course, but I probably shouldn't have. The officer who name-dropped you got a good glaring from her supervisor, and I didn't get anything more. They kicked me out after taking note of my investigator's license and telling me not to wander off, if you catch my drift."

"Where did you find Hari?" I asked. "His body, I mean?"

"In his apartment," said Kriggler. "A place called the Chesapeake Arms. Real run down joint. Small apartments, packed in tight. Not a lot of attention paid to ambience, if you catch my drift. A gamer haven. From what Sanika told me, I knew he'd retreated into that world to get away, but I didn't realize how far he'd fallen."

I wasn't surprised. "I was looking for a more specific answer, as in *where* within his apartment. In a gaming chair? Still plugged in?"

"That's right."

"A Princess Gaming unit?"

He shrugged. "I don't know. Probably. They're the company he had a subscription to, I think, and they're the main gaming company on Cetie, right?"

I nodded, stroking my chin.

"You want to share with me what you know?" said Kriggler. "As I said, the cops weren't terribly forthcoming, but I take it from the look on your face and the questions you're firing my way that you've been through a similar experience."

"Strikingly similar."

I gave him a brief run down, from Helena's appearance and hire of me to track down her estranged son to our investigation into Lars and the discovery of his death all the way through our online foray into his virtual existence. As I wrapped up my tale, I heard the puff of the front door. Carl stood there with a pair of reusable bags in his hands, one overflowing with leafy beet greens and the other sagging under the weight of assorted groceries.

"There you are," I said. "You didn't forget the buttermilk, did you?"

Carl walked in and paused near the sofas. "Joke all you want. You don't know how good you have it. I tried to get back as quickly as I could after Paige informed me about Mr. Kriggler, here."

Dirk shot a thumb at my old pal. "Who's this?"

"Carl," I said. "My partner slash caretaker slash best friend. Don't judge."

Kriggler shrugged. "Hey, no business of mine what happens behind closed doors."

I refrained from making a comment about him respecting the privacy of closed doors yet forcing his way though open ones. "You make it sound creepy. It's a platonic relationship."

"Rich," said Carl as he hefted the bags. "You want to help me put these away?"

"As if I'd know where everything goes," I said. "That's your job."

Carl shot a highly arched eyebrow my way. I got his drift.

"Right. Kriggler? Can I grab you something to drink while I'm up?"

The private eye removed his hat and set it down next to him on the couch, smoothing his disheveled hair with his fingers. I considered offering him a hot shave in addition to the drink, but he might take it the wrong way.

He leaned back and gave me a nod. "Yeah. Coffee. Black."

Of course. How else would a guy like Kriggler take it?

I followed Carl into the kitchen, where he indeed began unbagging groceries. I let him take care of that while I pulled a pair of mugs from a cabinet and set one of them under a shiny, copper spout. Despite my own self-deprecating jokes about my relationship with technology, I *could* operate the coffee machine on my own. I punched the start button and waited for the magic to happen.

"So," I said as Carl put the last of the milk in the fridge. "You wanted to talk?"

Carl closed the refrigerator door and cast a glance toward the living room. "How much do you know about this guy?"

"Kriggler?" I said. "Paige sent you the feeds, right?"

Carl nodded.

"Well then you know as much as I do," I said. "Claims to be a detective, which Paige confirmed, at least in terms of his official documentation. He's brash and forward and looks like he pulled his wardrobe straight from a historical vid doc on pre-millennial private investigators, something that might work on Cetif but makes him look stubborn and clueless here, but the story he's told about his client and current investigation are timely."

Carl frowned. "Exceedingly so."

The coffee spout sputtered and finished its business. I swapped out the full mug for the empty and started the process back up. "Are you saying he's lying?"

"No," said Carl. "Merely that his presence here is surprisingly coincidental. I think if you intend to work with the man, you owe it to yourself to be cautious."

I snorted. "I don't work in a team. We all know how well I fared during the last case."

"And yet you haven't kicked the man out," said Carl.

"Point taken. I'll keep my guard up."

When the coffee machine finished, I grabbed the pair of mugs and headed back out to the living room, Carl at my back. Kriggler sat where I'd left him, choosing to rest his backside rather than poke around in my medicine drawer. One point in his favor.

Kriggler accepted a mug as I held it in his direction. "Thanks, pal. So I was thinking about your yarn. This Busk guy, his death, his gaming habits, his online friends. The way I see it, there are two likely possibilities. Either the guy you found dead in his chair wasn't Busk, and Busk's out there living the dream, or you did find Busk, and someone's been impersonating him from the get go. At least for a period of years, if what you said is true."

I'd shared the details of my real life and digital investigations with Kriggler, but I hadn't primed him on my theories. "You came up with that by yourself?"

Kriggler looked at me like I might've lost a step in between the living room and the kitchen. "They're the only logical reasons why Busk, or the man impersonating Busk, could've been active online after his death."

I sat and took a sip of my brew, an espresso instead of Dirk's black. "So your victim Hari was a gamer. A heavy one, or at least he'd become one. Do you know what his online handle was?"

"Sure," said Kriggler. "DeadBeatdown13, which I'm sure he thought was either extremely clever given his family situation or was an expression of latent angst over the same. And before you ask, I checked while you were in the kitchen with your droid. He was last seen online about four hours ago. That matches closely to the moment his body was pulled from his gaming chair."

Perhaps it was Carl's cautious reminder, but I wanted to make sure of that tidbit myself.

Already on it, said Paige. *Looks like Kriggler's right. According to Princess's servenets, DeadBeatdown13 logged off a hair over four hours ago. Hasn't been on since. I also found the police report about the discovery of Hari's body. Not a lot of details available to the public, but it was at the Chesapeake Arms. No idea if Hari is DeadBeatdown, but Kriggler's story seems solid otherwise.*

I turned toward Carl. "So, let's look at the big picture. Two men die, apparently while gaming, apparently from similar causes. Malnourishment or dehydration or general lack of care of some degree. Both men seem to have passed away while maintaining virtual presences, and at least in the case of Lars, we know he was active and not merely online due to some glitch in the Princess servenets. If Dirk here tracked down the real Hari Gupta, then we have to assume the man we found in Lars's apartment is the real Lars Busk. Yet someone is out there impersonating both of them. Why? To what end? What do these two men have in common? What do they have worth taking?"

Carl didn't get a chance to respond, as Kriggler spoke right over him. "Did you check Busk's financials?"

I turned back to Dirk. "No. Why?"

The private dick gave me another condescending look. "I told you. My guy Hari had more debits than credits, and not just regular stuff like rent, food, and bills. His stipend check was being siphoned off. If our two marks are alike, than maybe you'll find a similar situation with your Busk boy. And if it so happens they're making payments to the same entity? *Bang.* That's your culprit. Bet you a thousand SEUs."

I felt sheepish. I should've made that connection. "Right. So where were his stipend payments going if not to his account?"

Kriggler cleared his throat. If it wasn't my imagination, his cheeks darkened ever so slightly. "Well...about that. I'm not sure, exactly."

I narrowed an eye. "Can't you check the bank records you obtained for Hari?"

Kriggler shrugged and sipped his coffee. "I may have overstated that. I didn't actually get any records. The lady I talked to was kind enough to relay some information to me, but she wouldn't give me the files. A breach of some information privacy act or other, she said. So I don't know where the money went."

"Wonderful..." I said.

"But," said Kriggler, undeterred, "I didn't have the same legal standing you do. Sanika and Hari had divorced long ago. Unless he'd secretly been married, which is highly doubtful based on everything you've told me, then your man Busk's next of kin would be his mother who hired you to investigate his passing—or his life, rather, but close enough. The point is, you have a stronger case to make to Busk's bank to give you his records than I did with Hari's."

"Despite working in this field, I'm not much of an expert when it comes to the law," I said. "Carl, is this accurate?"

He eyed Kriggler for a moment before turning his blues on me. "Mostly. You have a *stronger* case than Mr. Kriggler did, but Helena Busk will ultimately be the only one with authority to access Lars's accounts, including his records. If you're looking for an official statement of record, she'll be the one to have to pursue it. And I feel I should once again point out you haven't told her about her son yet. At this point, I'd be surprised if she hadn't heard from the police, but perhaps they're still waiting on confirmation from their DNA test."

I felt a pull at my heartstrings. "I know. I told you I'd tell her, and I will. Today. I promise. I'd still like to try and confirm Lars's identity through our own DNA test first, though."

"Then we should get to it," said Carl. "I don't feel right about withholding this information from her."

Kriggler sat forward, waving his free hand at us. "No, no. Forget that. That'll take too long. What you need right now is to contact the bank. Sweet talk them. Give them the old one-two. All we really need to know is if Lars's government work stipend was making it to his account, and if not, where it was going. We should be able to get that. I can talk you through it."

Carl gave me a wary glance. I took note, feeling a similar way.

"Look, Kriggler," I said. "Even if that's the path I wanted to take, I couldn't. I don't know which bank Busk did business with."

"Dang it." Kriggler stood and began to pace again, coffee mug in hand. "Well, there has to be a way to find out. We'll run some queries on the public servenets. Hack into his Princess profile. Something."

There's an easier way, said Paige.

I'm listening, I said, keeping the conversation to myself.

According to the Meertori building manager, Lars's apartment building takes payment by direct deposit. We greased his palms once. I imagine he'd be willing to talk again given another monetary incentive.

I'd already planned to make a return trip to the apartment complex to search for traces of Lars's DNA, so why not kill two birds with one stone? The only question was whether or not to include Kriggler.

I took a sip of my coffee and thought. Ultimately, curiosity won out over cautiousness.

"Grab your hat, Dirk," I said. "We're going to take a field trip."

18

Our car slid to a stop in front of a narrow skyscraper, at least a hundred stories tall but probably not more than twenty meters in width. A sheet of solid glass ran up its façade, gradually twisting along with the building to give the structure the appearance of a corkscrew. As the wall of glass spun, the side of the building became the front, almost as if the building turned its buttocks toward the wind, thumbing its nose at the elements the entire time. I gulped.

It's perfectly safe, said Paige. *With a width to height ratio of one to twenty five, it's nowhere near the skinniest high rise in Pylon Alpha, let alone the rest of Cetie. There's a seven hundred and fifty thousand kilogram tuned mass dampener up around the ninetieth floor that provides stability against seismic events, and that corkscrew appearance you're so worried about decreases shear loads from high winds by evening out the forces on the sides.*

Your scientific reasoning isn't going to do anything to assuage my acrophobia, I said as I stared at the structure.

Since when are you afraid of heights? said Paige. *You've never had a problem on the space elevator, or during flight-wing operation.*

The space elevator is attached to an asteroid orbiting Cetie, I said. *It's not going anywhere. And I wouldn't be worried about ascending this thing if I had a flightwing suit. Then I could fly instead of fall.*

"Hey? Can we move? Or are we going to sit here cooling our heels for the next half hour?"

I shifted my gaze inside the cab. Kriggler still sat in the seat across from me, for better or worse. I still hadn't determined which of the two it was.

After leaving my apartment, I'd travelled with Kriggler and Carl back to Lars's apartment complex. It took us a while to find the Meertori building manager as he didn't initially respond to the chime in the downstairs lobby, but eventually we located the guy napping underneath a stack of boxes in the back. Given the fact that we'd roused him from a peaceful slumber, I'd assumed he'd be less than thrilled to see us, but the exact opposite was true. His respirator obscured his smile, but its clanking and wheezing couldn't hide the eagerness in his voice. Likely he saw SEUs swimming through his eyes upon our approach.

Unfortunately for us, he'd improved his bargaining abilities. The information and access we'd been after didn't come cheap, but after a heated bartering session, my money ultimately spoke the loudest. Upon delivery of his promised payoff, the Meertor delved into his building's data files, procuring for us the name of Busk's bank. He also personally escorted us to Lars's room and let us in.

Miraculously, the contents hadn't been touched. I'd expected a guy of the Meertor's caliber to have gutted the place and sold the belongings within minutes of the cops leaving, so either the police had left specific instructions for him not to or I needed to revisit my faith in alienity. Either way, I was glad to have brought Carl with me, and not only because Kriggler's personality bristled with all the warmth of his native Cetif. Whereas it would've taken me ages to comb through Lars's carpets in search of a stray hair, Carl, with his various sensors and improved optics, was able to find one almost instantly. We'd packaged it and sent it to a lab for testing—but not before I broke down and admitted I needed to follow Carl's advice.

I made the call. Sharing the news with Miss Busk hadn't been easy, and her tearful response only made it worse, but I'd needed to do it, even if I couldn't yet confirm beyond a shadow of a doubt that her son was indeed dead. Honestly, she took the news better than I would've if I'd been in her shoes. After talking her through what I knew, she thanked me and told me she'd pay me for my efforts to answer lingering questions about her son's death. I graciously declined. The case had become something more to me than that. It always had been, more or less.

Of course, after that emotional exercise we still weren't any closer to discovering who, if anyone, had stolen Lars's identity, so with Kriggler hovering over my shoulder and coaching me as if I were a child, I'd called Lars's bank and demanded to speak to a live human. Eventually, the automated systems put me through to a lovely young lady by the name of Grace who did her namesake proud by putting up with my long-winded spiel and Kriggler's persistent interruptions. While she couldn't provide me with the actual records of his account, upon receipt of my contract with Helena and notice of Lars's death, she was at least able to walk me through many of his account details—namely that he, like Hari, was beyond broke and that his government stipend payments were being rerouted to a different account. Apparently, a bank by the name of Tau Ceti Consolidated Credit Corporation, or TCCCC, was now getting the payments. The whole thing sounded fishy, and not only because no self-respecting bank would fashion an acronym with that many C's.

So it was we found ourselves in the car outside the twisting, narrow high rise. According to the biz listings, TCCCC's Pylon Alpha office was located inside.

I waved my hand at the building. "After you."

The doors puffed open, and Kriggler stepped out first. Carl and I followed him, the Cetie heat blasting us fully in the face as we did so. I hazarded a glance at Kriggler as we walked toward the high rise's entrance, but other than a single trail of sweat weaving from his brow down to his collar, he didn't show any outward signs of discomfort. The guy was a rock. Perhaps extended exposure to Cetif's climes had frozen the rest of his sweat glands shut.

Together, we stepped into the lobby, a classically furnished space with lots of glass and brushed aluminum. A lovely blonde receptionist—a droid based on her lithe figure—sat at a wide, barely-there Pseudaglas desk, her legs crossed primly with her arms resting atop them.

Kriggler approached her. "Hi, doll. We're looking for the Tau Ceti Consolidated Credit Corporation."

She pointed to the elevators in the middle of the lobby. "Penthouse suite, floor one twenty one. Enjoy your visit."

"Thanks." Dirk nodded, gripping the brim of his hat as he tipped it toward the droid. I gave the lady a half-hearted wave and followed Kriggler.

A few folks milled about the base of the lobby as we waited, most of them dressed in business casual Hempette short suits or the occasional form fitting, vented Spandette power blouse for the ladies. A few of them joined us in the elevator, but they all exited on lower floors. After a long stretch of waiting, our lift dinged and spit us out.

The TCCCC had the floor to themselves. A sign with the company's name hovered over a doorless entryway, ushering patrons toward another receptionist's desk similar to the one from the lobby in size but thick, dark, and opaque, built from an expensive hardwood. Another droid stood behind it, tall, thin, wearing a crisp white suit jacket and a million SEU smile. He welcomed us with his demeanor, but as we approached him, it was the rest of the bank that caught my eye—and not for its opulence.

Apart from the reception desk, the place was thoroughly *mundane*. No exotic potted plants or free-standing fountains. No golden filigrees on the molding or finely carved statuettes. Not even any displays, holo or otherwise. But the office's minimalist nature went beyond the aesthetic. I didn't see any self-service kiosks, nor did I spot any staff, either tellers, investors, or managers, beyond the single, smiling droid in front.

A single door stood in the wall behind the droid, though I noticed a fire escape set into the wall at my far right. A low hum cut through the air, almost subaudible, but I felt it in my chest.

"Welcome to Tau Ceti Consolidated Credit," said the droid as we approached. "My name is Florian. How may I be of assistance?"

Once again, it was Kriggler who took control. "Hey, pal. Dirk Kriggler. This here's my acquaintance, Rich Weed. We're here to inquire about a couple of accounts."

"Kriggler and Weed," said Florian. "Hmm. We don't seem to have any Richard, Rich, or Ricky Weeds in our servenets. And is that Kriggler with two g's? Because if so, I'm afraid we don't have any of those either."

I secretly thanked the droid for his choice of stated nicknames. "We're not here for ourselves. Lars Busk and Hari Gupta. We understand they have accounts with you?"

"I'm sorry, sirs," said Florian. "But I can't share confidential information about clients, including whether or not we even retain certain individuals *as* clients. It goes against government mandated privacy rules for our sector. I'm sure you understand."

Kriggler glared at me. Perhaps I'd thrown a wrench in his master plan by revealing our victims' names too early.

"No, you, ah...misunderstand us," he said. "I'm an investigator. So is Rich, here. You process Cetie government stipend payments, don't you?"

"Of course, sir," said Florian. "As a fully licensed and accredited banking institution, we provide all our members with a host of services, including unlimited deposits, withdrawals, and transfers to and from other approved member institutions. Can I interest you in opening an account?"

"Cut the crap, bot," said Kriggler. "Busk and Gupta are dead. Their families hired us to investigate their passing. Each of their primary bank accounts had dipped into the red, but for some reason, both of them used your firm to process their government work stipends. So where'd that cash go, huh? Their families have a right to know."

"I'm sure they do," said Florian, his smile never wavering. "But as I already mentioned, I can neither confirm nor deny the identity of our clients, much less divulge any data regarding their financial transactions without a warrant—one delivered by an agent authorized to execute it, which despite your self professed status as an investigator, I suspect you don't qualify."

"Oh, this is about authorization? Why didn't you say so? Let me see here..." Kriggler reached a hand into his coat, digging for something—perhaps his investigator's license. "Ah, there we go."

He pulled back his hand. Steel flashed, and he leveled a pistol at Florian's chest, a combination pulse and projectile weapon with a narrow profile and a high density battery pack set in the grip.

"Dirk!" I said, taking a step back. "What the hell do you think you're doing? Put that thing away!"

Well, that explains the heavy coat, said Paige.

Carl held up his hands in appeal. "Please. Listen to Rich. Violence isn't going to solve anything. You have to realize that."

Kriggler kept his arm extended, the pistol gripped tightly. He glanced at me out of the corner of his eyes. "Shut up. You're the one who botched this confrontation in the first—"

Florian dove across the desk. Several things happened in concert. Kriggler's eyes widened. The bot swung an arm with superhuman speed. Kriggler mashed on the trigger. Shots rang out, brisk projectile cracks followed by electric crackles. Florian collided with Kriggler, and the pair rolled across the floor. More shots. More crackles. An alarm sounded from recessed speakers, and a bright red light began to flash above the elevators.

"Kriggler!" I said. "What the hell did you do?"

The private eye disentangled himself from Florian. The latter wasn't moving.

"He attacked me," said Kriggler. "He swung for my neck. You all saw it."

"Are you insane?" said Carl. "He's a droid. He's incapable of attacking you. He must've been trying to disarm you to prevent an accidental discharge."

"Bull crap," said Kriggler, holstering his pistol. "Check your feeds. That blow was going to hit me."

I opened my mouth to side with Carl, but Paige stopped me. *Rich. He might be right.*

The feed from a few seconds ago flashed in front of my vision. Florian, flying through the air in slow motion. His arm pulling back, swinging forward. The arc on it. The first of the pulse projectiles hit him, and his body jerked, sending his arm low into Kriggler's shoulder before impact.

I couldn't believe it. He must've planned on changing the trajectory. Bringing his hand down to grasp the gun.

I blinked, banishing the replay only to find Kriggler dragging Florian's frozen form across the floor to the door behind the desk. "Uh...what are you doing?"

The alarm kept blaring, and the light above the elevator continued to flash. "My pulse pistol put us on lockdown. I should've realized there might be a gunfire sensor in here, seeing as it's a bank. That's what happens when you get sloppy. But no point in wasting the opportunity. Should be a few minutes before police arrive. Give me a hand."

I glanced at Carl. He looked as lost as I did and possibly more morally torn.

Kriggler dumped Florian on the ground in front of the door, which blinked open. "Whoa. Proximity sensor. We're in luck. Must not be tied to the security alarm. Let's go."

"Where?" I asked, but Kriggler had already disappeared into the room beyond. Hazarding a glance at the elevator, I followed him.

Beyond the entryway, I found the source of the pervasive hum. A tightly packed servenet room, with only narrow corridors between the nets, each of them buzzing merrily. Vents at the top of the room blew cold air in, but despite their efforts, I felt a sweat coming on.

Kriggler knelt next to one of the nodes, a small electronic device in his palm. His eyes had glazed, but his fingers tapped efficiently at the device's display.

"Rich." Carl stood behind me. He nodded at Kriggler. "I think that's a skimmer."

I blinked. "What the heck is that?"

"Seriously," said Kriggler, his fingers still moving quickly. "What kind of PI are you?"

"One that adheres to the law," said Carl.

"Get off your high horse, princess," said Kriggler. "We're private. We do what we have to to get the job done."

"Maybe *you* do," said Carl. "We hold ourselves to a higher standard."

"Look, it's not as if I'm using it to steal people's personal information. I'm trying to solve what happened to Hari, same as you are with Busk." Kriggler stood and pocketed the device. "I've got what I need. Not everything, but a few hundred accounts, Hari's and Busk's included. Follow me."

He pushed past me and Carl, heading back into the reception area.

"Follow you?" I said. "Where? The elevators are locked down, remember?"

Dirk didn't respond, walking toward the fire escape. Amazingly, it opened in response to his touch. Either it hadn't locked due to some obscure fire code regulation, or Kriggler had teased it open with his less than legal gadget.

I raced after him, Carl behind me. "You're going to climb down a hundred and twenty-one flights of stairs to get away? Even if your heart doesn't give out, I think they'll intercept you at the bottom."

"I'm not headed down," he said. "I'm going up. The servenets were on a secure comm link, a line of sight transmitter of some sort. I'm betting it's on the roof if my skimmer's power draw sensors read it right."

The *roof?*

"Oh, hell no," I said. "I'm not going up there. You can help yourself to a windswept death if you so desire, but I plan on living for another century or two."

"Suit yourself." Kriggler hopped up the stairs, disappearing around a bend.

"I'll follow him," said Carl. "The police will want my visual feed in the event of a subpoena. Just don't do anything stupid to get yourself shot."

As if I'd do any such thing. Three minutes later, when the police burst through the elevator doors, pulse pistols drawn, they found me seated in the middle of the lobby, hands in the air and with a finger pointed toward the fire escape. I had no intention of becoming a statistic.

19

I sat on a hard, flat bench in the heart of Pylon Alpha's fourth district police precinct. Uniformed officers wandered back and forth in front of me, some with cups of coffee in hand, others with eyes partially glazed, taking Brain calls as they walked. They hustled about like ants, darting back and forth between conference rooms, holding cells, and each other's offices, all while the grunts in the main chamber before me guarded their cubicles, each flush with holodisplays filled with surveillance feeds, info tickers, and glimpses of the occasional strikeball match.

I turned to Carl, who sat beside me. "How long do you think this is going to take?"

He shrugged. "Could be minutes. Could be hours. It's bureaucracy. There's no way to know."

I groaned. "I don't understand why this is so challenging. I just want to talk to Kriggler."

"The police need to interview him thoroughly first," said Carl. "Get his side of the story and compare it to the security feeds. How long that takes depends on how eager Kriggler is to comply. It's possible he doesn't want to talk to you. He's not legally required to speak with anyone. Not even a lawyer."

"Psh. *Not talk to me.* As if anyone would willingly turn down that opportunity."

I sat there, tapping my fingers on my legs. I sighed. "I'll admit though, I'm tempted to leave him here. Let him fend for himself."

"Then why don't we?" asked Carl.

"It's not that simple."

"Curiosity killed the cat," said Carl. "Just saying."

"You know, I've never understood that expression," I said. "I've met cats. Were they curious, yes, but none of them had a death wish."

Did you know the expression actually began as 'care killed the cat,' said Paige, *with the first recorded instance appearing all the way back in 1598 in a play by the name of Every Man in His Humour. It wasn't until much later, toward the tail end of the nineteenth century that the expression transitioned to 'curiosity killed the cat,' though the exact origin of the variation is unknown.*

"Well that makes even less sense," I said. "How would a cat die being careful?"

Care as in worry or sorrow, said Paige.

"Well, thanks for adding that to the conversation," I said. "I'm sure that tidbit of knowledge will come in handy at some point in my life."

I'm in here with you, said Paige. *I can detect sarcasm.*

"You understand my point though, right?" said Carl. "There's no real reason for us to continue this investigation. We got the results of the DNA test back. Lars is who we thought he was. Let's hand over the rest of the information we gathered and let the police handle it."

I switched to an encrypted Brain feed for privacy. *You know there are two main problems with that. The information Kriggler gathered wasn't legally obtained, for one. The courts would throw it out, and the police can't investigate without cause. And the other reason is due to jurisdiction. This isn't purely a Cetie issue anymore. If Kriggler's data is right, we'd need to get at least one, if not more, Cetif PDs involved.*

If Kriggler's data is right, said Carl.

Do you have any reason to doubt it? We were right there with him the whole time.

Carl stayed silent.

I thought so.

While I'd stayed in the Tau Ceti Consolidated Credit Corporation's reception area and been taken into police custody, Carl had followed Kriggler up to the skyscraper's roof. Following Kriggler's skimmer signal, the pair had found a private satellite array connected directly to the TCCCC's servenet. Based on the inclination of the satellite array in the afternoon sky, Carl had guessed the thing was pointed at Cetif. Though Kriggler had chucked his skimmer over the edge of the building the instant the police arrived, he'd wirelessly transmitted the data to Carl before doing so. Since then, Carl had performed additional analysis of the servenet files and coordinates skimmed from the array. His silence now confirmed what we'd already discussed. Hundred if not thousands of Cetie bank accounts were being hijacked, their funds stolen, and the SEUs funneled through a secure channel to somewhere on Kriggler's home world. Questions abounded. How were the accounts being hijacked? The victims couldn't possibly all be dead—the deaths of Lars and Hari had to be coincidental—so how were the perpetrators hiding their tracks? Was it a simple cash grab, or something more nefarious? Who was behind it? And was it really our place to try and figure it out?

"Well, if it isn't Investigator Weed."

I looked up at the sound of a familiar voice. My buddy from Lars's crime scene, Oliver Sanz, stood in front of me with his arms crossed.

"Officer Sanz," I said. "I didn't realize you worked at this precinct."

"I don't," he said, a deep frown set into his cheeks. "The officers here called me in after you were taken into custody and your name popped up on a report regarding my investigation into the Busk death."

"Hopefully it was a short trip over from your office, then."

"Not especially."

Sanz stood there staring at me. I shifted on my seat, feeling the heat of his gaze.

"Okay, look, Weed," he said after a moment. "I don't know what your plan is, or what you hope to accomplish with this pal of yours, Dirk Kriggler—"

"Hey, now," I said. "That guy's not my pal, no matter what he says. I barely know him. He barged into my apartment a few hours ago. I only hooked up with him because our cases seemed to align. But I had no idea he was armed, and I certainly didn't know he was going to assault a droid. Seriously, I've done nothing wrong. I've complied with you guys from the get go, and—"

Sanz put up a hand. "I don't want to hear it. Trust me, I've already watched the security vids. If I or any of the other officers felt you should've been charged, then you wouldn't have been released right away. That's not why I'm here."

"Oh," I said. "Good to hear. Then why *are* you here?"

"For a friendly warning," he said. "I've been honest with you from the start. You haven't, though I thought you'd turned a corner during our last call. Now? I don't know what you're up to with this Kriggler guy, but I'd highly suggest you cool your heels and leave the police work to those with badges. From what you told me about your case, this doesn't concern you anyway. Speaking of which...we got the results of the DNA test back. It was, indeed, Lars Busk who died."

I nodded, not admitting we'd already learned the same from our own test. "Thanks for that. Anything else?"

"Yeah," he said. "Kriggler wants to talk to you. It's up to you if you want to abide by his request or not, but I've made my thoughts clear on the matter."

"Where is he?"

Sanz pointed across the room. "Holding cell sixteen. The security officer there will let you in."

I sighed. "I should at least hear him out. Carl? I'll be back in a minute."

I stood and crossed the common area, heading down a hallway and toward the holding cells. As I approached number sixteen, a panel flashed. Someone barked at me to identify myself, so I stated my name and pressed my thumb into the scanner when prompted. The gate opened and I stepped in. Kriggler sat behind a plain metal table in a chair of similar form.

"Rich. Buddy," said Kriggler. "What took you so long? Was it that Sanz guy? It was Sanz wasn't it?"

"I don't know what you're referring to exactly," I said. "And don't 'buddy' me. You don't know me. You certainly don't care about me. Buddies don't fail to mention they're packing heat and then pull said weapon out in public. They certainly don't fire on droids in the middle of a bank lobby."

"Rich, we talked about that," said Kriggler. "The droid attacked me. You saw it. It's on any number of feeds. The bank surveillance feed, your droid's, your own visual feed."

"Those vids are inconclusive to say the least. And if you think you're going to avoid charges by claiming self-defense against a *droid,* then you've lost your marbles. I don't know if Cetif's any different, but here and in the rest of the known universe droids are programmed *not* to kill humans."

"Stranger things have happened, pal," said Kriggler. "But that's besides the point. We have more important things to talk about—namely, our investigation."

I blinked and pulled up a chair, another folding metal one. It was as uncomfortable as I'd expected. "Are you not paying attention? You're here on assault and destruction of property charges. Be glad your pulse rounds only temporarily incapacitated that droid, otherwise you'd be facing far worse."

"I know what I've been charged with," said Kriggler, "and I think I can get out of all of it. But as I said, that's not important. Right now, we need to focus on you getting me out of here."

"Really?" I asked. "How do you plan on doing that? Did you manage to sneak a fusion-powered drilling laser in with you in your pants?"

"Don't be silly. You're going to bail me out."

I laughed, but the mirth died after a single guffaw. "And why would I do that?"

Kriggler leaned forward in his chair. "Because you want to know what's going on as much as I do. Because you made a commitment to your client, and you're the sort to see things through to the end. I can tell. Seriously, lives are on the line here. You'd follow this case even if you hadn't been hired in the first place. And last but not least, because you'll need me. I'm sure you've chatted with your partner, Carl. Talked about what he and I discovered. *Where it pointed.* Trust me, you'd be lost without me."

Kriggler was going out of his way not to mention Cetif, and with good reason. If the police had reason to think Kriggler would skip planet the moment he posted bail, they'd never let him out of their custody. Not that he'd make it very far. His name would automatically be added to every intra- and interstellar transportation company's no fly list. He wouldn't be able to buy a ticket, much less set foot on a freighter.

I shook my head. "It's a moot point, Dirk. Even if I post bail for you, we're stuck waiting for the due course of law. If you wanted to make progress on the case, you should've first thought about the repercussions of pulling and discharging your firearm."

"Come on," said Kriggler. "Help me with the bail. I'll pay you back. The charges aren't that serious. I've probably made more off incidentals from the Gupta case alone than you'll have to pony up. Just do it. Quick. The longer we wait, the colder the trail will get. You know that."

"I'll think about it. That's all I'll promise."

I turned and headed back out the gate, over to the common area, and back to Carl, who still sat on the bench. Officer Sanz had made himself scarce.

"Learn anything?" said Carl.

I took a seat. "Not really. Kriggler wants me to post bail. Wants to keep investigating, despite the obvious roadblocks in the way."

"Don't worry about what *he* wants," said Carl. "You don't owe him anything. The question is, what do *you* want?"

It was a good question. Ultimately, I wasn't sure. Despite the blunt and tactless way Kriggler had gone about his points, he'd made good ones. I'd always had a bit of a soft spot for maidens in need, and Lars's death had forced upon me a moral imperative to go above and beyond the line of duty in regards to Helena Busk. Not to mention the grander moral implications of our case. Kriggler's skimmer had found hundreds if not thousands of accounts being defrauded—presumably—of their government stipends. Two of those people were dead. How many others might be?

One thing was obvious. I couldn't sit on my hands and do nothing. Patience had never been a strong suit of mine.

I glanced at Carl. "I don't think you'll like what we're going to do next."

My partner lifted an eyebrow. "It involves Kriggler, doesn't it?"

"It involves money," I said. "A lot of it. Come on. Let's pay a trip to my bank. They'll want to be advised of this."

20

I leaned back in my captain's chair, plush white lambskin leather underneath me, sleek and clean and cool to the touch. A console swept out before me, a variable touch display trimmed in dark gray carbon fiber and loaded with the standard terrestrial controls and readouts: a speedometer, accelerometer, altimeter, geolocator, external pressure sensors, attitude indicator, and a host of other readings I'd yet to come to understand. Thankfully, I had Paige for that.

You've got me for all of it, she said. *As if you'd be able to pilot this ship without me. You didn't even know what attitude meant until I notified you ten minutes ago.*

I knew what it meant, I retorted. *Give me some credit.*

Oh, you knew what one of the word's definitions meant. Not the one related to geometry and orientation, unfortunately.

I lifted my gaze and looked out the front windshield, a wide expanse of Pseudaglas that might as well not have been there for all the optical interference it provided. Tau Ceti burned brightly in the sky outside, showering its warm rays over the vast reach of the spaceport's Epsilon runway before me. I couldn't even see the end, the pavement disappearing into the distance. I still wasn't sure why flight control had sent me to this particular runway. My Kestrel™ Chinook Z-Class didn't need anywhere near that far to achieve lift, or even to slow on landing. Maybe the other runways had been busy.

I called out over my shoulder. "Carl? How are we doing on everything? Provisions? Fuel? Are we good to go?"

I heard his footsteps as he approached from behind. "It's a little late to be asking that, don't you think? We're *literally* waiting for final takeoff approval."

"Sorry," I said. "I feel like I should be calling out important questions and commands to the crew, like 'batten down the hatches,' and 'check the resonant cavity thrusters for gravitational lensing!'"

Carl sat next to me in the copilot's chair. "You're just throwing words together now, aren't you? Do you have any clue how this ship works?"

"On a grand scale, yes. At the micro level? No."

Don't worry, said Paige. *Carl and I have you covered. As always... And for the record, yes, I made sure to check the food stores and liquid hydrogen tanks as part of the several hundred item long pre-flight checklist. You won't lack for snacks, and we won't run out of fuel. Of course, even if we did, we wouldn't be stranded. This vessel is equipped with a Bussard hydrogen scoop. We could putter along on stray atoms until we found a spot to refuel.*

"But we wouldn't be able to land anywhere," I said.

Depends on the atmospheric composition of the planet we're trying to land on, said Paige. *Assuming said planet has an atmosphere. I'm assuming most of the ones we'll be visiting will. Congrats for knowing what a Bussard scoop is, by the way.*

"Eh. I inferred it from context."

Carl smiled and shook his head.

"Are you laughing at me?" I said.

He looked up. "Me? No. Well...a little. I'm more surprised to find myself here. In this ship, specifically. I really didn't think you'd pull the trigger on the Chinook."

"But you're glad I did, right?"

"Well, I'm glad you didn't blow your entire fortune on a broken down used freighter, if that's what you mean," said Carl. "That isn't to say I fully approve of the purchase. Or of everything else..."

The intercom crackled to life. *"Fhloston Paradise. You are cleared for takeoff."*

I breathed a sigh of relief. Given the delay, I'd started to worry. "Thanks, flight control. Paige?"

I'm ready to engage the engines as soon as you buckle yourself in.

I glanced at my chair. "Right."

I did as Paige asked, and she sent power surging into the thrusters. A rush of acceleration mashed me into the back of my seat. The runway blurred, and before I knew it, we'd surged into the sky. Trees and cars and buildings shrunk beneath us, and our acceleration slowed to a more moderate level.

I paused with my hand over the seat restraints. "Paige? Is it safe to unbuckle?"

I'm no flight attendant, she said. *This is your ship, remember. Do what you want. But if you're asking for my flight plans, I intend to keep the Paradise on her current trajectory for another eighteen minutes or so. Once we start to clear Cetie's mesosphere and enter the thermosphere, I'll reorient us for a deep space burn. We'll continue to experience Cetie's gravitational field throughout, though, so you shouldn't have anything to worry about.*

"Good. Carl? Give me a hand."

I unbuckled and headed into the back, dropping down a ladder from the cockpit into the Chinook's common room, a surprisingly airy space equipped with a pair of wraparound bench and table sets, retractable lounge chairs with built-in holoprojectors, and a kitchenette at the back. I ignored the lot and headed to the middle, crouching down over one of the floor panels.

I held out my hand. "Carl? Electromagnetic clamp?"

He searched under his coat and produced two of the handle-like items in question. He handed me one and crossed to the opposite side of the panel. We each pressed our clamps into place against the panel and activated the current.

"Ready?"

Carl nodded.

"On three."

I counted, and we lifted. The panel slid free, revealing a flat gray slab of metal underneath, its surface coated with ice crystals and held in place by an equally frosty latch.

Carl and I dumped the panel to the side, then I crossed back over and undid the latch. I knelt, gripped the edges, and lifted, throwing the box top open.

"Still alive in there?" I asked.

Dirk Kriggler uncurled from a fetal position, slowly standing and stretching himself back out. Frost crusted his jacket, and ice crystals sparkled in his hair. He pulled an oxygen respirator from his face and glared at me.

"Was that *really* necessary?" he said.

"Maybe, maybe not," I said. "It all depended on whether or not we got selected for a random walkthrough or infrared scan before takeoff. As it turns out, we didn't, but there was a moment there when I thought flight control was going to call us back."

Kriggler dumped the respirator on the ground and climbed out of the smuggling compartment. "I don't care the reasons. I'm not going back in there."

I frowned and crossed my arms. "I'm detecting a distinct lack of gratitude here. Did the cold addle your brain? Because it seems as if you've forgotten that I didn't have to bail you out. I also didn't have to drop a cool five million SEUs on this brand new Kestrel spacecraft so we could fly to Cetif on a private vessel, thereby hurdling your police-issued travel ban, and I didn't have to get it equipped with a secret smuggling compartment before takeoff. You act like getting you off planet was easy. Heck, I wouldn't even have known where to get the compartment installed if I didn't have a former smuggler turned bounty hunter friend who was able to pass along a guy's name. Besides, from everything I hear about Cetif, you should be right at home in the cold."

"It rarely freezes there," said Kriggler. "We get a consistent, chill drizzle more than anything. But I suppose you're right. I appreciate the help, pal. I owe you. Big time."

Wasn't that the truth! Not only did Kriggler owe me monetarily for his bail and the cost of his passage onboard my new ship, but he owed me for my loyalty. I could've easily left him behind and continued the investigation on my own, but I figured his expertise would be the only thing keeping me from running into a brick wall the instant I set foot on Cetif. Even Carl had agreed, surprisingly enough. Even though I was fairly sure he disapproved of the journey entirely, once he saw I'd set my heart on travelling to Cetif, he insisted we bring Kriggler, despite the unlawfulness of it all. Maybe my old partner was getting rebellious in his advanced age.

"I'm not sure if that's an apology," I said, "but I'll take it. Now help Carl get this panel back in place and strap up. You don't want to be standing when the ship undergoes its course correction and transitions to a constant linear thrust."

21

Rain pattered off our car's panoramic Pseudaglas roof, the droplets fat and heavy and shimmering with the reflected light of several dozen blue, green, and magenta holosigns. They flashed intermittently, cutting through the cloud-shrouded dark of the Cetif night with stylized caricatures and symbols of bottles, cards, dominos, and barely clothed ladies. Real women dressed in similar fashion, probably frozen to their toes but somehow shrugging it off, stood under floating umbrella drones on the street corners, puffing on methamphetamine wands. Light from the signs played off the rain-slicked carapaces of Diraxi enforcers who stood in the shadows behind them, tall brutes with abnormally large pincers and an aura of violent indifference.

Our car pulled into an alley. The tall, looming walls on either side of us cut out even the colorful gleams of the holosigns, casting our car into shadow. We pulled ahead in silence, the faint electric whirr of the motor barely audible under the soft drumming of the rain.

After a moment, we pulled into a courtyard, one with dull black pavement and metal trashcans taking the place of trees and grass. A heavy, steel door stood closed against the side of one of the buildings, illuminated by a bright red diode above it that cut through the gloom. A group of fifteen to twenty individuals clustered under an awning to the side of it, sequestered behind a length of cord strung between posts.

"This is it," said Dirk. "Tiger Paw Number Five. Hottest bar in Lower Melghat."

Apparently, Lower Melghat was the name of the cesspool into which we'd ventured—at least according to Kriggler, but Paige backed him up, and I trusted her fully if not necessarily him. Not that it was much worse than the rest of Cetif we'd thus far seen. By my estimation, everywhere we'd travelled since parking the *Fhloston Paradise* in one of local spaceport's hangars had been dull, gray, and unseemly.

That's an unfair assessment, said Paige. *The planet wouldn't even be livable without those persistent clouds that turn the world dull and gray.*

And I suppose the copious numbers of gambling establishments and strip clubs are all part of Cetif's global temperature regulation efforts, too?

Paige didn't respond. Neither did Carl, who sat next to me.

"Tiger Paw Five," I said to Kriggler. "Got it. Remind me again what we're doing here?"

"We're looking for a woman by the name of Daayan," he replied. "No last name. No first name, either, for that matter. Daayan translates to witch, or something along those lines. Seems insulting if you ask me, but that's the name she goes by. Far be it from me to question her on that."

"And why do we need to talk to her?"

"Because unlike the jacket we picked up for you at the megamart, you can't buy skimmers off the rack," said Kriggler. "I need a replacement for the one I pitched off that high-rise on your home world before we can continue tracking the signal from the satellite array. Besides, Daayan has her ears to the ground. If someone's funneling large quantities of SEUs from Cetie bank accounts, she'll have heard about it. She might not be willing to hand the information over, but she'll part with it for a price. Anything can be bought with her."

I glanced at my new coat, a solid black ElastoLeather jacket I'd chosen partially for its warmth and partially because it was one of the few things that fit my short, muscular frame. I'd also sprung for matching, ultrathin ElastoLeather gloves, a new pair of lined pants, and a rather stylish dark gray field cap. Despite packing what warm clothes I'd had, I'd been woefully unprepared for Cetif's weather, both the cold and the rain. Shade drones weren't particularly useful when the wind started to blow water droplets at you sideways.

Kriggler opened the door and headed toward the club's entrance. I exited after him with Carl bringing up the rear.

With the rain hammering down on our heads, Kriggler pounded on the door and stepped back. After a moment, the door swung open. A big bruiser with a crop of buzzed black hair, probably a meter ninety and a hundred and forty kilos, stomped out.

"There's a line for a reason, folks. I told you I'd call when—Kriggler? Is that you?" The brute narrowed his eyes.

"In the flesh, Jack," said Dirk. "Miss me?"

Jack's face, if that really was his name, darkened. "You've got a lot of nerve showing your face here after—"

"Hey, now, that brawl wasn't my fault and you know it," said Dirk. "Now, work with me. I need to see Daayan. She in?"

Jack snorted. "In her usual corner." He lifted a thick finger. "But if I hear even a hint of a shadow of a scuffle—"

"There'll be hell to pay, I know," said Kriggler as he pushed past him.

"We're, uh...with him," I said, unsure if I really wanted to associate myself with Kriggler.

Jack stared at us, jaw clenched. I hustled forward, thinking I could probably outrun him if push came to shove.

I followed Kriggler inside, down a narrow set of dimly lit stairs and toward a curtain at the bottom. Music thumped rhythmically, becoming louder with each step, the bass notes compressing my chest with their power. The curtain rose and fell, and I stepped into the melee.

Lights pulsed, purples and blues, pinks and yellows, oranges and greens, cycling, rotating, and flashing as they played over a ceiling of glassy metal droplets. People danced and ground to the beat, a psychedelic repetitive rhythm, some sort of post-traditional fluorescent magneto-dub. The air hung thick and heavy, as much from the dancers' sweat slicked bodies and volatilized perfume sprays as from the humidity outside.

Kriggler plowed into the crowd, and it took everything I had not to lose him. I plunged in after him, feeling strangers jostle against me, hopefully with platonic intentions. The music flowed, as did we through the crowd. Eventually, the sea parted, and we found ourselves in front of a VIP area, cordoned off by sound-cancelling privacy curtains. Kriggler headed toward one in the back, pushing through without pause. I followed.

Inside the curtains, which cut down the sound of the pulsing beats by a considerable margin, I found a table and padded velvet benches. Two large men with tan skin and thick beards stood at the sides of the entrance. On the bench sat a woman with a slightly lighter complexion, thick eyebrows, smoky eye shadow, and iridescent purple locks held in place by hair sticks.

She blinked. *"Dirk Kriggler?"*

With lightning-quick speed, she pulled a pulse pistol and aimed it at Dirk. The guards pulled guns, too. Dirk pulled a pair of pistols from inside his own jacket—from where, I wasn't sure. I figured the police on Cetie had confiscated his gun, but apparently he'd managed to hold onto it and another to boot.

I slowly lifted my hands. "I...uh...guys?"

Kriggler shifted his guns between the two guards and the woman with the purple hair. "Daayan. Good to see you haven't lost your speed. How have you been?"

The air crackled with anticipation. One of Daayan's eyes narrowed. I gulped.

With the same speed with which she'd pulled it, Daayan slipped the gun back under the table. Her eyes shot open. "Kriggler! You old son of a gun. Have a seat. Introduce me to your friends."

I eyed the goons as they returned their pieces to their coats. "Well, friends might be stretching things a—"

"Shut up," said Kriggler as he holstered his own pulse pistols and took a seat. "This is Rich and his android buddy Carl. They're investigators from Cetie."

"Ah, yes," said Daayan, leaning back and stretching her arms over the edge of the bench. "I'd heard a rumor you'd left us."

"Heard any other rumors?" he said.

Daayan shrugged. "I have excellent hearing, but my tongue rarely wags. It makes me a poor conversationalist but a superior businesswoman. So what took you to Cetie?"

"Work." Kriggler eyed me. "Seriously. You heard the lady. Have a seat."

I nodded, still amazed I'd avoided being shot. I slid onto the bench across from Kriggler, scooting in to give Carl some room.

"So," said Daayan, turning to me. "You're in the same line of work as Kriggler? Were you dropped on your head as a small child?"

"If I was, you could blame Carl here," I said. "For all intents and purposes, he raised me. But in all honesty, it's not a bad gig. The pay is hit or miss, but the work is fun."

"You enjoy it then?" asked Daayan.

"Most of the time," I said. "Depends on the job."

"That's great," said Daayan with a smile. "Now why the hell are you here?"

"I lost my skimmer while in the line of duty," said Kriggler. "It, uh...fell a few hundred meters and shattered. I was hoping you might be able to provide me with a new one."

"Happy to help," said Daayan. "Ten thousand SEUs."

"*Ten thousand?*" said Kriggler. "For a skimmer? Are you crazy?"

"I'm not running a charity, here," said Daayan.

Kriggler snorted. "I'll give you seven and a half."

"Ten," said Daayan. "If you don't like it, you can buy one from any of the other underworld commodities traders who don't hate you for previous offenses. Oh... Right. There aren't any."

Kriggler grumbled. "Fine. Ten. You own me, though."

"I really don't," said Daayan. "Not after how you stiffed me the last time."

"Account information?"

Daayan sat there and stared at Kriggler. His eyes flicked. She must've sent him the information via Brain.

"Alright," he said. "We're good."

Daayan's own eyes flicked. "Happy to do business with you." She nodded to one of the goons. "Raji? A skimmer."

He nodded and exited through the curtain, letting a burst of rhythmic thumping through in his wake.

"So," said Daayan. "Are you going to tell me what this is all about? A case that takes you off planet and brings you back with a pair of investigators in tow? Must be something big."

"It might be," said Kriggler. "You want to refund me part of my purchase price?"

Daayan sniffed. "I get paid for information, not the other way around. Besides, I thought this could be more of a barter situation. You tell me what you're into and I tell you what I know that could be of use to you."

Kriggler gave me a nod. "What do you think?"

Honestly, I was just happy Kriggler hadn't asked to borrow ten thousand SEUs from *me*. "Couldn't hurt. It's not as if we have much to go on other than that satellite signal."

"It should be enough."

"And what if it isn't?"

Kriggler chewed on his thoughts. He eyed Daayan. "Someone's funneling funds from Cetie here on a private comm linkage. Government work stipends mostly, but it's enough to clean out the accounts. Ripped off both of our clients, which is how we met. The perp seems to be targeting folks who die of natural causes and won't be missed—at least, that's the theory I'm working off of. I don't like the alternative."

Daayan lifted an eyebrow. "When you say funds...how much are we talking about?"

"Quite a bit," I said. "Kriggler skimmed data from the servenets of the shell corp processing the payments. There's at least hundreds of accounts. Perhaps thousands. Could total hundreds of thousands of SEUs per month. Depends how long the con has been ongoing."

Daayan's brows furrowed. She didn't say anything.

Kriggler cleared his throat. "This is the part where you chime in with something useful."

"You're not going to like it," said Daayan.

"Try me."

The woman took a deep breath. "There've been rumors circulating of a hacker by the name of Guy Sharp. A pseudonym, undoubtedly. Word is he's raking SEUs in by the bucketful, but nobody knows how. Nobody's had their drug, prostitution, or racketeering enterprises impinged upon by a newcomer."

"How is that bad news?" said Kriggler. "Off planet SEUs could explain all of that."

"I haven't gotten to the bad part yet," said Daayan. "Word also has it Guy's spending a lot of those SEUs on illicit arms. Apparently, he's building a private army, but again, there hasn't been any word of mercenary hires. Perhaps he's only getting started."

The goon returned. He held a skimmer out in an oversized hand.

Kriggler took it. "Thanks. Think Dundu might know about this?"

Daayan smirked. "What do you think?"

"Who's Dundu?" I asked.

"An old friend of mine," said Kriggler. "The underground sort."

"You have friends?" said Daayan. "That's news to me."

"Hey, you welcomed me with open arms."

"I figured it would be worth my while," she said. "And it was. But we're done now. So kindly remove your ass from my bench and show yourself to the exit."

"Please," said Kriggler. "Don't shed any tears."

"I'll do my best. Try not to die." Daayan eyed me. "You, too. You seem nice enough, which means you're more likely to croak. Feel free to come by if you need anything. I'm always open for business."

She gave me a smile, and I wondered if there was any double entendre to that last bit. I'd never been into unnatural hair colors, but the purple worked with her smoky eyes and exotic good looks.

Carl elbowed me in the side, and I moved before I did anything that caused the goons to pull their guns again.

22

The rain had stopped when our car pulled up in front of a narrow storefront, one with a flashy holosign out front proclaiming it to be 'Dundu's Novelties and Imports.' The place next door had been shuttered, and a two meter tall rotating green credit slip advertised a pawn shop across the street.

I exited the cab and followed Kriggler to the shop's door, which opened upon his approach despite the late hour. I couldn't help but notice an obvious camera situated above the door, pointed directly at us. It could've easily been replaced with a much smaller, more subtle version, but perhaps subtlety wasn't the point.

A chime sounded, announcing our presence. Inside, I found a wide assortment of wares. Shelves full of delicate porcelain and shiny silverware, colorful accent rugs, pillows, candles, wide wicker chairs, and oil diffusers— not at all what I'd expected given the neighborhood. Several of the candles burned, filling the air with scents of cherry blossoms and mountain dew and sending shadows dancing across the aisles. A counter in the back stood empty.

Carl and I lingered at the front while Kriggler approached the counter, calling out, "Dundu? You here, Dundu?"

Carl leaned in close to me. "I don't understand why we're here. Dirk was able to relocate the signal from the satellite array using the skimmer he procured from Daayan. We should be tracking the signal's origin, not wasting time on unnecessary stops."

"He also said he'd only be able to narrow the signal's landing spot to a five kilometer radius," I said, "which isn't too bad given the distance between here and Cetie, but that's not going to be good enough to find this Sharp guy. Or Guy Sharp. Whatever. Either way, I'm guessing there's a reason for our presence here. Something tells me Dundu isn't simply a mild-mannered trinket salesman."

Kriggler had refused to say who or what exactly Dundu was, but if I had to speculate, I would've pegged him as another informant, some member of Kriggler's vast web of eyes and ears, almost friends and pseudo enemies.

I heard a voice carry over from the back. "Do my eyes deceive me? Dirk Kriggler, is it not? What a lukewarm, pleasing surprise."

I poked my head around a shelf. My eyes confirmed what my ears already suspected. Dundu was a Tak.

The bovine alien trundled forward, his hooves clattering on the flooring as he walked. He waved with one of his stunted arms, the hands and fingers far too small for the rest of him by human standards but perfectly in line with the average for Taks. He flashed a creepy, toothy grin as he approached the counter, his ears perking. All together, it gave him the appearance of a cow all too eager to be milked.

"Good to see you, Dundu," said Kriggler. "And I'm glad to see the feeling's mutual. I was worried after, you know...the *Saladrius* incident."

The Tak waved it off. "A brush with death. A momentary lapse of reason. All in the past. Said event caused a great increase in sales, let me assure you, so I hold toward you no infirm conscious action."

I think he means ill will, said Paige.

Right. Taks were notoriously poor comprehenders of human turns of phrase.

Kriggler looked back. "Rich. Get over here."

I walked forward and gave the Tak a halfhearted wave. "Hi. Rich Weed. Nice to meet you. Cool place. Lots of porcelain."

"All hand painted," said Dundu. "By Tak hands, you understand. Much smaller, much finer than human hands. This makes quality much improved over the alternative."

"I'll take your word for it," I said. "You don't have any problem getting around the store with all of it around?"

The Tak's ears flattened. "What do you imply? That because I am large and quadrupedal I am poorly coordinated? That my wide posterior is a veritable magnet for fired clays?"

I should've known the guy wouldn't get my bull in a china shop reference. "No, I wasn't implying that. I—"

Dundu broke out in a loud, braying laugh. "Hah! I jest, of course. I have knocked numerous bobbles and bowls to the floor over the years. My fingers, they are composed of congealed milk fats."

"Dundu," said Kriggler. "Let's talk business. My friend and I are in the market for some of your wares. I owe him, financially speaking, from a little run in with the police, so it'll be my treat. I can vouch for him."

"Ah," said Dundu, steepling his fingers before him. "By all means. Let us peruse the goods."

"No offense, Dirk," I said, "but I'd rather you Brained me the bail funds directly. I don't have interest any in hand painted china, even if I didn't have to drag the plates back to Cetie on the *Paradise*. No offense, Dundu. I'm sure they're wonderful."

Kriggler turned and looked at me with furrowed brows and narrowed eyes. Despite the obvious physiological differences, Dundu managed to give me a similar look.

He shrugged it off quickly, waving at Kriggler. "Come. I will show you."

He led us around the counter, through a door, and into a storage area filled with stacks of the same merchandise as in the front, most of them wrapped in thin layers of clear packing plastic. We stopped in front of a corrugated metal wall.

"We have arrived," said Dundu.

I wasn't impressed, but I tried to hide it. "Uh...nice wall."

I heard a clank, a grind, and a whirr. The metal panel lifted, revealing a dark space behind it. Lights flickered to life inside, revealing an arsenal of the likes I'd never seen. Pulse pistols, projectile pistols, and combo units. Rifles of the regular and sniper variety, combat shotguns, grenade launchers, railguns, and deployable drone turrets, all hanging from racks, on hooks, and on the walls.

"Holy crap," I said under my breath.

"So," said Dundu. "What can I forge interest in you with?"

"We don't know what we're up against," said Kriggler, stepping forward to browse through the weapons, "so we'll need to remain as flexible as possible. That means combo pulse projectile pistols for everyone. Except me. I've already got a pair. But I'll take a couple tactical rifles, the ones with flight correcting tracer rounds—oh, and ballistic vests and pads for good measure. Maybe some smoke mines and EMP grenades, too."

"Whoa, whoa," I said. "Pistols, I get. Rifles? Mines? Grenades? What the hell do you plan on getting us into?"

"You heard Daayan. Sharp is building an army. Better to be overprepared than dead." Kriggler grabbed a pair of pistols and threw them my way. By some miracle I caught them before they hit the floor. I didn't want to test the safeties yet.

"Did you say Sharp?" said Dundu. "As in Sharp Guy?"

"Guy Sharp, not Sharp Guy." Kriggler paused. "Oh, Dundu. Don't tell me..."

"His representative came bearing copious amounts of SEUs," said Dundu. "What was I supposed to do?"

"No, it's okay," said Kriggler as he hefted a large pulse rifle from its home. "This is good. You can tell us what you sold him and how much. You said his lackey came to you? Did he load up a truck, or did you deliver?"

Dundu wrung his hands together. "I am unsure if I should say. He purchased many weapons. I do not wish to be positioned on his rotten half."

"Come on," said Kriggler. "Remember the *Saladrius*? You yourself said business boomed afterwards."

"Yes. *Boomed*. Exactly." Dundu made an exploding motion with his hands.

"Just tell us Dundu. I'll make it worth your while."

"Fine," he said. "Mostly pulse weapons were purchased. A mixture of pistols and rifles. No body armor. No explosives. But many weapons, so do not say I did not share the warning."

"Good. Dispersive vests it is, then." Kriggler picked out a few more things and brought them back. He handed me a vest equipped with a mixture of spare batteries, clips, and grenades. He held a belt equipped with a pair of pistols in Carl's direction.

Carl took the weapons hesitantly. "You realize I'm a droid, don't you?"

"Nobody said the mercs would be human," said Dirk. "Dundu. You didn't answer my second question. Did you drop the guns off yourself or not?"

The Tak nodded. "I did. A factory of some sort, not more than twenty minute's drive from here. I can provide an address, if necessary."

"Twenty minutes?" said Kriggler. "That should be within the signal radius. Jackpot."

"*Jackpot*?" I said. "Are you *nuts*? You're talking about walking into a situation where we virtually *know* we'll be encountering a firefight."

"We'll be expecting it," said Kriggler. "They won't. That gives us an advantage. Now strap that vest on."

"You're kidding, right?" I said. "I'm supposed to wear this in public? What if we get pulled over by the cops?"

Dundu brayed again. "Hah! His residence is not within close proximity, is it?"

"He's a Cetiean," said Kriggler. "Dundu? What do I owe you?"

"I have your account information," said the Tak. "I will withdraw the correct amount through the proper channels. Very subtle, as usual. I simply hope the payment does not return unfulfilled. Dealers of arms are not individuals to be fleeced."

"I can cover it," said Kriggler. "At least I think I can. Weed. Mount up."

"Oh, one moment," said Dundu. "Because I care about you and your continued business... Before you leave, take some stimpacks. On the home, as you would say."

"*Stimpacks?*" I said. "What is this, a video game?"

"Perhaps I used an improper term," said Dundu as he rifled through a bin. "Injectable pharmaceuticals, tailored to your particular physiology. A mixture of blood coagulants, stimulants, and painkillers. Perfect for the modern urban mercenary on the go."

"Dundu's right," said Kriggler. "We'll take some. Could come in handy if the situation deteriorates."

I paused and pressed a hand to my temple. Pulse rifles? Body armor? Stimulant injections? I couldn't believe what I was getting myself into.

Might as well do it, said Paige. *I mean, we've come this far, right?*

I glanced at Carl. He shrugged, as if to say he'd join me, whatever my decision.

I sighed. If Carl and Paige were on board, who was I to say no? "All right. Let's do this."

23

Our car pulled through an open gate and slid to a stop in front of a towering factory. Spotlights bathed the cooling towers in cool blue light, some of which trickled down to the pavement outside but precious little. It was almost as if the building's designers cared more for ambience than nighttime safety. Then again, based on the barren nature of the parking lot outside, I suspected the factory only operated during daylight hours—if at all. That would be a point in our favor.

Kriggler cracked the door and hopped out, a tactical pulse rifle hanging around his neck from a strap. He glanced at the skimmer in his hand.

"We're smack dab in the middle of the radius," he said, "and my signal strength is as strong as ever. I think we've found the place."

Wonderful... I hopped out after him, feeling the weight of the energy dispersive vest over my chest. For perhaps the first time, I was appreciative of the cool weather. Whereas here the armor merely bothered me, on Cetie it would've unleashed on me a tidal wave of sweat or, at worst, been the instigating factor in a debilitating case of heat stroke.

Dirk slipped the skimmer into one of the many pockets on his vest. He pointed. "That looks like the front doors. Let's check to see if they're open."

"Right," I said. "And if anyone asks, we're members of the Lower Melghat SWAT, investigating a call about a bunch of heavily armed gang members."

Kriggler snorted. "Again with the police jokes. As if they were going to show up. You crack me up."

I glanced at Carl, who'd also exited the cab. "You ready?"

He wasn't wearing a vest, but he'd strapped the belt into place. His coat mostly hid his pistols, so at least *he* didn't look like a threat to public safety. "I'll bring up the rear. You follow Kriggler."

Dirk set out across the barren stretch of pavement separating us from the factory doors, his rifle held at the ready. I kept pace with him, a cool breeze picking up and bringing with it another hint of rain. Somewhere in the distance I heard a siren. The factory itself emitted a low, electronic hum, but other than that we travelled in silence.

We neared the doors, but they didn't open upon our arrival. Kriggler pushed on them to no avail, then pressed up against a window and peered inside.

"Can't see much. Too dark." He tapped on the window with the butt of his gun, but it didn't seem inclined to give. Probably Pseudaglas.

"There must be some way in," I said. "Maybe if we look around..."

Carl walked over to the side, coming to rest near a large set of metal slats. He knelt and pointed to a latch system on the side. "Rich. I think this door is activated manually. And it doesn't appear to be locked."

"No way," I said.

Carl stood, crossed to a recess in the middle, and pulled on it. It slid up and in, rattling along on slider wheels.

"See?" said Kriggler. "Luck's on our side. Let's go."

He dove into the opening, and I reluctantly followed. Bits of light trickled down through enormous skylights onto the factory floor, illuminating tall cranes and presses and conveyer belts in blue outlines. I didn't trust myself not to smack into smaller barrels and crates, so I activated the tactical light on my rifle. Through its cone of light, I spotted huge blocks of light gray plastic sitting next to extrusion presses, the sparkle of electronics and multi-colored wiring, and bundles of pistons, actuators, and power supplies that had been assembled into limbs. Looked like a low-level droid factory.

Kriggler activated the light on his own rifle. He waved at me to follow before taking off at a jog. With my weapon gripped tight, I moved through the factory floor after him, waving my flashlight to and fro. Large machinery loomed at me out of the darkness. Some cranes stood empty, tall and proud and ready for action, while others held hulking metal containers and canisters in mid air as if they'd been stopped mid-shift. Steel ladders stretched into the rafters, providing access to a pair of long hanging bridges that hung over the factory floor. Red LEDs blinked intermittently from deep within the gloom, all while the factory pulsed with its omnipresent electronic hum.

Kriggler stopped and glanced at his skimmer twice, changing direction each time. Eventually, we worked our way to the factory's far side. There, a trio of sliding metal doors similar to the one through which we'd entered stood open, revealing more of the blue-tinted gloom outside. A drizzle had once again started to fall, slicking the surfaces of a number of delivery vans and heavy transports parked there.

Kriggler paused just inside the doors. He pulled the skimmer from his pocket and glanced at it again. "Well, I've got good news and bad news. The good news is I'm positive this is where the satellite array is pointed. The bad news is I can't pinpoint where the signal is being retrieved. I suspect there's another receptor array on the factory roof. We should try to find a way up there. Either that or look for a servenet room. If we can find the latter, I should be able to tap back in and see if the funds we're after are being rerouted to a conventional account."

I listened to Kriggler with half an ear, all the while wondering who'd left the loading doors open. Sure, the parking lot was empty, but to leave the front doors unlocked and several loading bays in back open seemed exceedingly careless, especially for someone who might well be engaged in illegal activities. Besides, the neighborhoods we'd travelled through to get to the factory didn't exactly give the impression goods left unattended would still be there in the morning. Still, the factory seemed abandoned, of transients, thieves, and security. Why?

I noticed a crate sitting outside next to one of the delivery vans. Its top lay open, collecting rainwater, and it appeared to be empty. I lifted my rifle and shone my light on its side, illuminating the words 'Dundu's Novelties and Imports.'

"Kriggler." I nodded toward the crate.

He looked up from his skimmer. "Yeah, so? Dundu already told us what he delivered. Did you expect they'd leave a big box of weapons sitting around?"

I didn't, but I *did* wonder what had happened to said weapons.

"Rich?"

I turned at the sound of Carl's voice. I found my partner staring into the factory. A moment later, I heard what had undoubtedly drawn his attention. The clatter of footsteps.

I suddenly became keenly aware of my tactical vest and rifle. I suffered an urge to hide the latter behind my back, but thankfully, I realized how silly that would be before I tried it. Kriggler's and my intentions would be obvious from our apparel. Better to keep my weapon at the ready in case I needed it.

Emboldened by the fact that I hadn't already been shot at, I called out. "Hello? Who's there?"

The footsteps continued. A moment later, a figure emerged from the darkness, gleaming and plasticized. A low level droid, of the sort businesses employed for repetitive, non-service related jobs with minimal human contact. It possessed the same height and build as Carl, but it lacked his exterior finishes: hair, skin and tissue substitutes, or even clothing. Based on the parts I'd seen on my trek through the factory, I'd bet he'd been manufactured here.

The droid's eyes flicked to my weapon. "State your purpose."

So much for pleasantries... I opened my mouth, but I realized I didn't know how to respond to the demand. How could Kriggler and I have planned an impromptu raid on a factory without coming up with a plan for what to do when confronted? Sure, *police* might not arrive, but what about the other forces we might encounter, the ones we were actively tracking. It seemed like a major oversight on our parts.

"You are not authorized to be here," said the droid. "Leave at once."

The droid took another step forward. Something at his side gleamed in the dim light, not his hip but at that height. It looked like...*a pulse pistol.*

Kriggler turned. "No can do, pal. We need access to your local servenet. Now you can make this easy and take us there yourself, or we'll do it the hard way and find it by trial and error. I assure you, the latter involves a trail of potential destruction that you won't want to have to explain to your masters. So...what's it going to be?"

The droid's eyes shifted to Kriggler. It could've been my imagination, but it seemed as if he was looking at his hands. His skimmer.

The droid's arm blurred as it tore the pistol from its side. It whipped up. Two electric crackles split the air. A pulse round, sparking and hissing, flew up from the tip of the droid's gun into the rafters as the droid himself flailed and fell backward. He slammed against the hard factory floor, his body still.

Carl stood next to me, his own arm extended, pulse pistol in hand.

I blinked, trying to understand what had just happened. "He... He..."

"Would've shot you if I hadn't done the same to him first?" finished Carl. "It would appear that way, yes. Either that or he's a terrible marksman, something I find extremely unlikely given his synthetic status. Besides, if his systems were functioning properly, he wouldn't have fired anywhere near you and Mr. Kriggler."

"I... But..."

Dozens of lights flickered and blazed to life inside the factory. The whirr and clank of heavy machinery began to sound, but behind it, there was something else. A rolling drumbeat. A cascade of synthetic feet hitting the hard floor.

Kriggler hefted his weapon. "Folks. We've got a problem."

24

A herd of droids materialized from behind a conveyer belt fifty meters away on the factory floor. Carl grabbed me by the vest and threw me into the shadow of a stamping press as a flurry of pulse rounds crackled and hissed, ripping through the air like a swarm of angry bees. Kriggler dove in the opposite direction, rolling and taking cover behind a control station for the loading bay doors. He knelt and poked his rifle out around the edge of the station, cutting loose with a burst of combo rounds.

Carl joined in the fray, taking his place at my side, peeking around the side of the press, and filling the air with pulse rounds. The steady *rat-tat-tat* of Kriggler's rifle and the irregular crackle of Carl's pistols fought against the buzzing hailstorm of the droid's shots. A few clanks and thumps sounded from out in the distance, but I couldn't tell whether they were from droids crumpling to the floor or from factory equipment lurching into motion. I refused to stick my head out to look.

Kriggler pulled his gun back, his back pressed against the control panel. He waved his hand over his shoulder, gesturing toward an elevated room in the middle of the factory from which lights now blazed. "We need to stop the factory's machinery, otherwise we'll be overwhelmed in no time. I think we'll find the controls in that tower in the center. I'll go left and work my way up through the interior. You and Carl head right. Draw fire. You should be able to take the elevated walkways. Meet me there."

"Stop the factory's machinery?" I said. "*Are you crazy?* You can't possibly think this is an assault droid factory, do you? Kriggler!"

It was no use. He'd already popped up and darted off to the side, spraying a cloud of fire toward the droids' position as he did so. Return bolts plinked and sparked as they impacted the floor in his wake.

Carl kept firing. He spared me a quick glance. "Anytime you want to pitch in and help, feel free."

I pressed a hand against my forehead. "This is insane. *A battle droid factory?* That's impossible. An inability to bring harm against humans is a core component of android programming."

"Well, these particular droids are firing on us," said Carl, "and I don't think they're doing it out of love."

I glared at him. "Sarcasm? Really? You're taking this surprisingly well."

Carl leaned around the corner and shot a half-dozen more rounds. "I'm dealing with reality, Rich. The droids are here. They're shooting at us. That's a fact. I don't know how, but we'll figure it out later. Daayan said Sharp was a hacker. He bought arms from Dundu. The pieces are all there. Right now, my focus is on keeping you alive, and to that end, I could *really use some help.* You're the one with the rifle and grenades, after all."

I blinked. I still couldn't believe it, but Carl's point rang true. If I didn't get my ass into gear, I wouldn't have time to figure out the details later.

With my rifle in hand, I stood and spun, unleashing a flurry of combo rounds in the direction of the conveyer belt. The droids had closed on us since I'd last seen them, but that only made it easier to spot them. A few fell under my muzzle's fury, but I crouched back down once I'd spied their position. Ripping an EMP grenade from my vest, I activated it, counted to two, and chucked it over the stamping press. I heard a clack as it bounded once, then a bright blue flash warped around me, bringing with it an audible whoosh like that of a car passing at high speed. The hairs on my arms stood on end, and the sound of metallic bodies hitting the floor soon followed.

I glanced at Carl. He stood, his back pressed against the press, his eyes wide and his arms shaking slightly.

"Please be careful with those," he said. "And for the love of science, tell me before you throw one."

"Sorry. Got it. What's the plan?"

"Kriggler's right," said Carl. "We need to draw fire away from him. Chances are we'll find controls in that elevated room. Let's head to the walkway ladders. I'll cover you as you go up, then vice versa."

I swung my rifle over the edge and fired off a few more shots. "Are you sure? Even assuming we can get up there in once piece, we'll be sitting ducks."

Carl shrugged. "The walkways look to be steel. It's conductive, and you're wearing boots and a dispersive suit. You should be fine. Besides, we can use those elevated containers for cover. I think I see some boom controls up there."

"Boom, as in crane, or boom, as in explosive?"

"Rich, this is *not* the time," said Carl. "Move! I'll cover you."

I spotted the nearest ladder off to my right and took off at a run—or at least as close as I could get in a half-crouch—sprinting from drill press to extrusion press to stack of crates as pulse rounds rained down around me. Somehow I made it to the ladder without being shot, though my heart threatened to tear through my chest from the overabundance of adrenaline flowing through my veins.

Carl raced only a step behind me. "They're looping around behind us, and I spotted more ahead. Looks like they're coming right off a line. No time to waste. Go! I've got you."

Carl kept firing. I jumped onto the metal ladder before my nerves got the best of me. I flew up the rungs, my Cetie-strengthened arms and legs giving me an off-planet boost.

It wasn't enough. A pulse round slammed into my chest. It sparked and crackled, raising goosebumps over every square centimeter of my body. Luckily the dispersive vest did its job. My grip never loosened, and other than the split-second shock of impact, it barely slowed me.

I grunted as I pulled myself onto the walkway. I immediately pressed myself against the railing, poked my gun through a gap, and fired a few score combo rounds toward the factory floor. Droid faces poked haphazardly through the machinery. I might've even struck a few, but I didn't put too much stock in accuracy. I had enough ammunition strapped to me for an hour's worth of target practice, and I didn't care how many of the attackers I brought down. If Kriggler was right, no amount would be enough.

The ladder rungs clanged, and Carl hopped over the edge onto the walkway next to me. He punched his finger into a touchpad at the edge of the railing, and a large shipping container suspended by a crane in midair lurched forward, tracking the edge of the walkway.

"They're coming in hot," said Carl. "You take point. I'll bring up the rear. Use the container for cover while we can."

I banished fear from my mind. Action gave us a chance at success. Hesitation didn't. I rushed forward, firing more shots off the side of the walkway where the shipping container didn't shield us. Pulse bolts shot up at me like a bizarro world rainfall, hissing and buzzing as they dissipated against the mesh walkway or impacted the factory's ceiling.

My rifle cracked. My feet pounded. The walkway crackled. Carl shouted.

"Rich! Look out!"

I lifted my head to find another crane-suspended shipping container swinging in from the side, meters from the walkway.

I swore. The container collided with the walkway. Metal screeched and tore, twisted chunks of it raining down. I jumped, but not before the side of the container slammed into my body armor.

I wheezed as the air left my lungs. My rifle spun from my hands, flying out into the factory. I desperately grasped for purchase as the impact sent me soaring. By some miracle, I wrapped a few fingers around the edge of one of the cables suspending the container.

I gripped it tight, but the container swung wildly from its collision with the walkway. Its momentum carried through me, wrenching on my arm. My shoulder screamed. My chest burned. I couldn't breathe.

"Rich!"

I felt a shudder. My fingers loosened. I couldn't hold on. My grip slipped.

Carl appeared over the edge of the container, grabbing my arm as my fingers gave out. He pulled, and I flew over the edge onto the top of the metal box. Carl lay on top, his legs wrapped around one of the support cables.

I tried to thank him. It came out as a wheezy groan.

"Watch out," said Carl. "We're coming back around."

The container had completed its arc and begun to swing back toward the far side of the walkway. The part we'd jogged along had collapsed, but the rest still stood, providing access to the control room. If we could jump to the walkway on the return swing, we'd have a clear path. The question was, did Kriggler send the container our way, or had it been the attack droids?

Tough to say, said Paige. *On the one hand, the container could've killed you. On the other, it's made it virtually impossible for the droids to follow you along the walkway.*

Paige, I said. *You're alive. I'd almost forgotten about you.*

I tend to stay quiet when my host body is in mortal peril.

Carl grabbed me. "Jump!"

We swung over the walkway, barely missing a second collision. Carl pushed me over the edge of the container. We slammed into the mesh with enough force to smash the breath from my lungs, but I still hadn't filled them with air from the last collision. As more shots plinked and sparked around us, Carl helped me to my feet and dragged me forward.

"Come on, Rich!"

Regular me would've complained, but air starved, psychologically and electrically shocked, didn't-have-a-death wish me could only nod and run and hope not to be turned into a public service announcement about the dangers of high voltages.

The door to the control center stood firm before us. We raced forward and smashed through it, collapsing to the floor of a space filled with windows, displays, digital and manual controls, and an array of servenets. Kriggler crouched inside the room's other door, firing rounds from his rifle into the opposing stairwell.

"You made it," he said. "Quick, take over here at the stairs. Hold them off."

Carl nodded and took his place as Kriggler crossed to the servenets and produced his skimmer. I peeled myself off the floor, checked to make sure I hadn't lost any limbs, and took position across from Carl. I'd lost my rifle, but a pair of pistols still hung from my belt.

I managed to draw one as the first wave of droids appeared in the stairwell. I fired a few rounds, but Carl's superior aim took care of most of them first.

"Tell me something good, Kriggler," I said.

"I'm in," he said. "Just looking for the factory master controls. Wait...here they are. Give me a sec..."

Usually such a statement was hyperbole, but a bare second later, the clanks and whirrs of the factory began to slow, fading to the building's original pervasive hum except overlaid with the sounds of angry droids and intermittent gunfire.

Another few droids mounted the stairs. Carl and I downed them with precision shots.

"Kriggler, what else have you got?" I said. "Is this the place or isn't it?"

"It's the place," he said. "The bank accounts from Cetie are being routed through these servenets. But I've got bad news. I don't think Sharp's here. I found another relay transmitter, a short distance one with a smaller reception radius. It's a weaker signal than I'm used to, intentionally weak I'd guess, and it's encrypted, but I might be able to track it to its origin. At least close, anyway—assuming I can decrypt it."

The droids had stopped running up the stairwell, so I glanced at the displays over the windows. Several featured security vids from the premises, including one of the loading docks. A swarm of droids gathered there.

"You might not have to do any of that," I said.

Kriggler looked up from his skimmer. "How's that?"

I nodded toward the display. The droids had split into six groups and were heading toward the vans. "Looks like our attackers are making a break for it. Call it a hunch, but I'd guess they're retreating to a safe house."

"Well then, what are we waiting for?" said Kriggler, stuffing the skimmer back into his vest pocket. "I've got what I need. Let's move before they get away."

Kriggler took off down the stairs, and I didn't hesitate, heading right after him. Adrenaline surged through my veins, infusing me with unbridled power and confidence, and my guns sang out, ready to continue the fight.

25

I miscalculated. I assumed there would be enough vans to go around, but the last of them pulled away as we raced through the loading bay doors and into the cool night rain.

"Paige, quick," I said. "Call the car from the other side."

"No time," said Kriggler. "We'll take one of the heavy transports."

Dirk darted toward one of the big rigs, vehicles designed for hauling goods, not people. Still, they could move, and though they lacked creature comforts, they'd contain an access panel and display in the front storage compartment for user access.

Dirk threw open the nearest rig's side door and climbed in. Carl and I jumped in after him. In no time flat, Kriggler had rushed to the front panel, whipped out his skimmer, and started the motor. A pair of rotors in the chassis whirred to life, and we lurched into motion.

The acceleration almost toppled me. It clanged shut the truck's side door, sending us into near darkness, held back only by the shine of Dirk's skimmer.

"Kriggler?" I said. "Lights?"

"On it."

LED strips lit up along the edges of the transport's interior, bringing to life the bland metal walls and streamlined ceiling. Another push of acceleration sent me scrambling for purchase.

"I'm going to need some sort of feedback on directional changes," I said. "This whole no windows, no displays rig interior isn't exactly helping my balance."

"Just a sec," said Kriggler. "Giving you Brain access to the transport's feeds."

Got it, said Paige. *Let me see what I can do. How about I apply a fifty percent translucency filter to the images cobbled together from the transport's external cameras and superimpose it over your visual feed? That should help.*

Paige performed her magic, and suddenly, everything around me appeared to be made of a clear plastic, not just the cabin but the truck's wheels, engines, battery packs, and sensors, too. The road blurred under my feet, dangerously close. The hairs on my arms rose in trepidation, but at least I could see the turns coming.

I steadied myself against a wall as we pulled onto a main thoroughfare and surged forward. Rain smeared against the cabin exterior as we accelerated, and the flashy roadside strip joint and pawn shop holosigns turned into colorful streaks. Because of the late hour, we had the road to ourselves—except for the pair of delivery vans I spotted out in front, perhaps thirty to forty-five seconds ahead of us.

"How's it looking, Kriggler?" I asked.

He looked up from his skimmer. "How's what looking?"

"The signal," I said. "I'm assuming we're following those vans, so how's the signal faring? Was I right?"

"Too early to tell," he said. "We look to be headed the right way, but it all depends where those vans go. I'm still trying to decrypt the data I skimmed from the factory servenet, so I'll keep an eye on the signal strength and keep you posted."

"Good. I've had enough of being yanked around. It's time to find this Sharp guy and end this once and for all."

Our truck continued to accelerate, closing on the vans. Streetlights blurred as we streaked past. Rain pattered against empty sidewalks, having driven even the purveyors of drugs and sex inside. I counted the seconds by which we trailed the vans. Twenty. Fifteen. Ten.

"How close do we want to get?" asked Carl.

"What do you mean?" I asked. "As close as possible. We can't lose them."

"We also don't want them to know we're tailing them," said Carl.

"We let that cat out of the bag around the time you shot the first droid," I said. "There's no way they don't know what we're up to."

"Then perhaps we should ask ourselves where we're going," said Carl. "If they know, they won't be taking us to Sharp's hideout."

"Kriggler?" I said.

"Still tracking toward the source," he said.

Carl frowned, and while Kriggler's assertion justified my position, I couldn't help but wonder if Carl had a point. By my count, six vans had departed the factory ahead of us. So where were the other four?

Rich?

Yes, Paige?

I might have an answer for that.

I turned. Two of the vans had materialized behind us. Despite our own impressive speed, they seemed to be closing on us.

"Uh-oh," I said. "Carl? Maybe we should prepare for—"

Wheels screeched as a van exploded from a side street and rammed our truck in the side. Metal bent and groaned. I flew through the cabin, impacting the truck's far side and once again having the air knocked from my lungs. The truck wheels swerved underneath me as the back of the rig fishtailed. It swung perilously sideways, the wheels spinning over the rain-slicked street. The cab began to tip, and I held what little breath I had left.

Two wheels lifted and hung in the air before the truck fell back down, skidding and screeching and wobbling as it reoriented itself.

I groaned and tried to stand. "Kriggler! Get this thing under control, will you?"

"You think I'm driving?" he said, half sprawled on the floor. "I'm just telling it where to go."

"Well, keep her steady! Do something!"

I turned to find one of the vans behind us had closed to within a few meters. It shifted lanes, heading left to our undamaged side, accelerated, and pulled up alongside us. The side door opened and rolled back on sliders, revealing a jumbled mass of droids within. Most of them still clutched pulse pistols, but one in front held something much larger—a cross between a fire hose and a grenade launcher.

My brow furrowed. "What the...?"

The droid pulled back on the weapon's handle, and a cloud of droplets shot against the side of the truck, obscuring my vision. A moment later, it blazed to life, and I felt a searing heat radiate towards me.

Carl grabbed me and threw me toward the front of the cabin. "It's a thermite sprayer! Get back!"

The wall started to dissolve, filling the air with caustic smoke and a thundering hiss. Somewhere over the ruckus I heard Kriggler shout out. "I've got it! I cracked the encryption! We're headed the wrong way."

"Well, redirect us," I shouted. "Now!"

Our truck swerved. I slid across the cabin floor into the front right corner as we curled left, all as the side of the truck disintegrated into a shower of sparks and molten metal.

The van alongside us barreled into us as we turned, sending up another cloud of sparks alongside a grinding metallic screech. Droids flew into the truck cabin, stumbling and falling from the collision. Carl and I unloaded our pistols, turning them into hunks of scrap before they had a chance to turn their weapons on us.

Carl ran back, continuing to fire shots into the van. The vehicle, now battered and bruised, shuddered and slowed as a flurry of rounds penetrated its motor compartment.

The other van trailing us swerved out of the way to avoid hitting it before speeding up to take its place. The side door rolled open, and I took cover behind the remainder of our truck's side panel to avoid the subsequent shower of gunfire.

"Kriggler," I shouted. "Let's pick it up!"

"Trying," he called back. The truck surged once more, and I almost lost my footing.

The droid van kept pace, speeding up to match us. Suddenly I heard a screech of brakes, a number of blares, and a scream. I turned forward to see a half-dozen cabs in front of us.

Finally we'd encountered traffic. Unfortunately for them, a forty thousand kilo truck traveling at a hundred kilometers per hour presented an unsolvable physics problem. Our truck crashed through the assembled cars, sending two flying and toppling me to the floor but barely slowing us down.

The van swerved once again, but the droid operators were too quick. They somehow avoided crashing, losing only a bit of speed before catching back up with us. Through the semi-translucent truck wall, I saw the droids part to make space for another one equipped with a thermite sprayer.

"Rich," said Carl. "I don't know how much more structural damage this thing can take."

"Got it." I grabbed one of the EMP grenades from my vest and activated it. "For the record, this is your official warning."

I leaned over the side of the hole and chucked the grenade. Somehow my aim and timing were both true. The missile flew straight into the van and erupted nearly on contact. Blue light flashed, and I felt the same whoosh of compressed air as before, but this time a ferocious blast immediately followed it. The van exploded in a fireball, sending high velocity shrapnel and bits of flaming thermite spraying in all directions. The blast knocked me to the floor.

Kriggler cried out. *"Argh!* Son of a..."

I looked up. A patch of the thermite had burned through the wall, landing on Kriggler's arm. Already it had disintegrated his shirt and left a vicious wound in its wake.

"Dirk!" I said.

Kriggler grimaced as he dug one of Dundu's injectables out of a pocket and stabbed it into the affected area. Almost instantly, the blood flow lessened, and Dirk's grimace eased. "It's alright. I'll be fine. We'll take care of it later."

Pieces of car continued to rain down behind us as we flew along the street at high speed. I couldn't believe I hadn't heard the high-pitched wail of a police siren yet. If that hadn't attracted them, what would? A tactical nuke?

"Status report on location," called Carl.

"Almost there," said Kriggler, glancing at his skimmer. "Reload your weapons. Keep them ready. Who knows what we'll find at Sharp's base."

Our truck slowed, swerving and turning as it carried us into seemingly darker and drearier streets. Within minutes the urban blight turned to slums and the slums to shanty towns. Not even shady pornographic holosigns filled the air anymore.

"Hold tight," said Kriggler. "We're coming in hot."

The truck slammed on the brakes, skidding to a halt in front of a dilapidated tenement. Kriggler, oblivious to his gaping arm wound, jumped out light as a feather, skimmer in one hand and pulse pistol in the other.

"Follow me! Go, go, go!"

Kriggler smashed through the front door and into the apartment complex. Shadows loomed deep and thick within, intermittently banished by weak, flickering lights.

Kriggler surged forward, and I followed. My heart beat like a drum, but my senses felt piqued, alert, superhuman. My gun had become an extension of my arm. Droids jumped at us from the shadows, and I downed them with perfectly timed, precise shots. Sweat rolled down my forehead and slicked my palms, but my grip didn't loosen. My technique was flawless, my arms burning with lactic acid as much as satisfaction.

Down the hallway. Around a corner. More darkness. More droids. More shots fired. My gun sang. My heart soared. I roared with power.

"This is it!" shouted Kriggler.

Another door imploded under the force of his shoulder, flying inward in a half-dozen pieces. Inside, a man sat before a bevy of panels. He shot to his feet and spun at the sound of our entrance. A pistol flashed in his hand.

A shot rang out. The man fell, clutching his chest. I turned.

Carl held the pistol, pointed straight at him.

26

The man crumpled, blood seeping onto the floor of the grimy, single room apartment. Carl stood there, pistol arm perfectly still and mouth agape.

I couldn't believe what I'd seen. "Carl. You...shot a man."

Carl's jaw moved, but it was a moment before any sound came out. "I... I...thought he was a droid. We'd seen so many, had so many come out of the shadows at us. I reacted instinctually. Rich...I don't know what happened. I never would've— Heck, I couldn't have—"

The man gurgled and coughed, and I ran to his side. In the heat of the moment, I hadn't seen what sort of round Carl had fired, but upon approaching him, it was obvious a projectile had been involved. Blood pumped freely from a wound in his chest. His face had already paled, and his eyes had started to glaze.

"Carl!" I called. "This man needs medical attention. CPR. Something. Quick!"

Carl stood there staring into the distance, completely immobile. I'd never seen a droid in shock before, but then again I'd never seen one shoot a human either.

I ripped one of Dundu's stimpacks from my vest and injected it into the man's chest. The injector puffed and clicked as it delivered its payload, producing a wheezy gasp from the man. Unlike Kriggler's thermite toasted arm, the blood flow from the man's wound slowed but didn't stop. I wasn't a master of anatomy, but the pistol round looked as if it might've pierced one of the man's lungs, perhaps hitting a major artery.

"Kriggler," I said. "Help me out here!"

"Me?" Dirk crossed over and knelt next to me. "What do you want *me* to do?"

"I don't know," I said. "Help. Medically. You've got that skimmer."

"It's a hacking tool, not a portable surgical bot."

"Well, do *something*," I said. "Call the paramedics."

The man wheezed again, and his eyes started to roll back.

I smacked him lightly on the cheek. "Hey. Stay with me. Guy? Guy Sharp? Can you hear me? You're going to be okay."

The man's eyes focused slightly, presumably at the mention of his name. He coughed, and a bloody foam sputtered over his lips, collecting at the corners. His chest contracted in pulses, and I thought he might be having a seizure—at least until I heard the grim resemblance of a laugh on his breath.

"Hah. The...j—jokes on...you."

Kriggler pressed his skimmer to the man's fingertip.

"Hey," I said. "What are you—"

The man kept going, though his voice was fading quickly. "You'll never c—c—catch him. He's t—t—too smart. Too f—fast. Three...steps...ahead. Always."

"Catch him?" I said. "Who? What are you talking about?"

"Just a...pawn," said the man as his eyes closed. "Just...a pawn."

The man's head rolled to the side, and his breathing stilled.

I slapped him on the cheek again. Once. Twice. Three times. "Sharp? *Sharp!*"

"Forget it," said Kriggler. "He's gone—or at least he will be by the time the medics arrive. There's nothing more we can do."

"Nothing we can do?" I glanced at Carl, who still stood there, unflinching. His arm had only now started to lower. He blinked several times as if he wasn't fully sure where he was. "How can you be so cavalier about this? A man is dead, and his blood is on our hands."

"Guy Sharp is dead," said Kriggler as he moved to a small servenet cluster under the displays in the corner. "So forgive me for not shedding tears over a degenerate hacker and wannabe mercenary overlord."

I glanced at the dead man. "He's Sharp? You're sure?"

"Ninety-nine percent," said Kriggler. "I ran his prints. His face came up along with a number of aliases, one of them a Sharp variant. He's a known hacker, with dozens of hacker associates on file. But..."

Kriggler paused at the servenet cluster, skimmer in hand. He stood there for a moment, then swore loudly and slapped one of the displays with his free hand. "Damnit!"

"What?" I said. "What is it?"

Kriggler sighed and turned to face me. "He's not our guy."

I blinked and shook my head. "What do you mean *he's not our guy*? You just said you confirmed he was Sharp. You tracked the rerouted signal here, didn't you? How could he not be the guy?"

"There's another router here," said Kriggler. "Looks like the Cetie funds, as well as additional Cetif funds, are being relayed back off planet again. I'm not sure where yet. Possibly outside the solar system if previous trends hold. There could be multiple relays, multiple endpoints. That's what Sharp must've been getting at before he died. He's not behind this. He was a pawn. There's someone else at the helm. Someone one step further up the ladder."

I stood and pressed a hand against my brow. I couldn't fully wrap my head around it. We'd broken into a bank, risked imprisonment by skipping bail, travelled half way across our solar system, fought off an army of custom-made, psychologically-hacked battle droids, and survived a high speed death race only to find out our Guy wasn't *the guy*. How could it be? And where was all the money going? Hacked Cetie accounts routed off planet to fund illegal robotics programs and gun running, all before being rerouted off planet again? It was a tangled web of conspiracies wrapped in a plot and sprinkled with mystery.

I glanced at Sharp, dead on the ground in a pool of his own blood. Carl still stood where he'd entered. He glanced at me with sorrowful eyes.

I turned to Dirk. "So, what you're trying to say is...the princess is in another castle."

"Pardon?" said Kriggler.

"The princess is in another castle," I said. "It's an old gaming trope. It means the object of your desire isn't where you expected it."

"Yeah," said Kriggler. "I guess. Something like that. Look, Rich. This isn't over. Whoever's behind this? We're going to get him. We're going to track him down, whatever it takes, and—"

I whipped my pistol from my side and leveled it at Dirk's chest, checking the mode selector on the side with my thumb to make sure it was set in projectile mode.

Kriggler threw his hands up. "Whoa! Pal! What are you doing? Put the gun down."

Carl suddenly found his voice. "Rich? Calm down. What's going on?"

"Who are you, Dirk?" I said. "What the hell's going on here?"

"What are you talking about?" said Kriggler. "I'm a PI. Now put the gun down. I'm on your side!"

"Like hell you are," I said. "Ever since you showed your face outside my apartment, things haven't been as they should. A private eye from Cetif? Paige said it checked out, and I believed her, but everything else? You drew me along at every step. Laid out the ground-work for us to have one and only one path to follow. You were the one who pulled your gun at the bank, who shot that droid. *You* passed along data to Carl that pointed us toward Cetif, data *you* skimmed from those servenets. But it doesn't end there. Once here we met *your* friend Daayan, who gave *you* a new skimmer. Then it was off to *your* friend the arms dealer. We followed *your* skimmer to the warehouse, and then once you decrypted the data, *you* sent us here."

"Because I'm the one from Cetif, and I know how to use the skimmer," said Kriggler. "Look, Rich, I know it's hard to accept, but that's how it goes sometimes. Thieves are smart. Conspiracies can be big. You have to follow them to the end."

"No, you don't," I said, my pistol hand as steady as granite. "Not when everything you've gone along with makes zero sense. Battle droids? *Really*? As Carl pointed out, you don't question reality when it's trying to kill you, but I don't care how good a hacker Sharp was, there's no *way* he was able to program droids to attack humans. That's the most fundamental, basic subroutine in android Brain architecture. He would've had to transform the way droids are created at the most elementary level. No one in the history of mankind has ever succeeded at that.

"But that's not it, is it? It's not even half of it. Between the droid battle at the factory and the high speed van chase and the thermite sprayer explosion that covered half a city block in ash and slag, you seriously expect me to believe Cetif police wouldn't come *check to see* what's going on? That injectable did wonders on your arm yet somehow did little for Sharp. And what about myself? I've had firearms training, but not much. Not with tactical rifles, not in high pressure situations, and yet—screw modesty—I've turned into a legendary purveyor of droid death. As has Carl, who I should mention has never fired a weapon in his existence."

"He's an android," said Kriggler. "He doesn't need practice. And you should show some gratitude. He saved you from countless droids. Over and over again."

"Not just droids," I said. "He shot a man. Carl. Carl, *an android,* shot a man. With lethal force."

"Rich, I told you," said Carl. "I thought he was a droid. I don't know what happened..."

"Stop it, Carl," I said, not taking my eyes of Kriggler or moving my gun. "Don't you *dare* try to reason your way out of this. Your decision making is instantaneous. You don't make mistakes, not without external stimuli, and you certainly don't make them when a human life is on the line. You shot a man. And then what? You stood there. You did nothing. You know first aid. You know CPR. It's a fundamental element of your programming. And yet you did *nothing.* Even if you *had* somehow made a mistake, if the gun had misfired, if a stiff breeze had pushed against your trigger finger— you would've helped Sharp. You would've tried to save him. The Carl I know would've. He wouldn't have stood there, helpless and shocked."

"It was Sharp," said Kriggler. "He hacked the droids, Rich. He must've hacked Carl, too. While we were at the factory. A remote program must've uploaded a worm into his subroutines."

"In real time?" I said. "Without him noticing? Give me a break. No. I think it's something else entirely. Something more nefarious. I don't know who's behind it, but I intend to find out."

"More nefarious?" said Dirk. "What do you—"

My pistol rang out. Kriggler gurgled and stumbled back as blood spurted from his neck. He flailed and spasmed before falling across the displays. Within a moment he'd gone still, blood flowing from his neck, across his vest, and dripping down onto the servenet cluster beneath.

I stared at Kriggler's body, slowly lowering my pistol. Nothing happened.

"Rich?" said Carl. "Good heavens. *What have you done?*"

I swallowed hard. "Not enough apparently. I'll see you soon, pal... I hope."

Before Carl could do anything, I turned the gun on myself and pulled the trigger.

27

I squinted as I cracked my eyes. A white room swirled into focus around me, with bright lights shining down onto me and an array of gleaming metal and plastic instruments lining the walls. A white sheet covered me to my chest, and an assortment of small white tabs had been pasted to my arms. I think I felt more on my chest and temples. A bag of intravenous fluids hung from a stand at my side, slowly dripping through a catheter into the vein at my arm, all while a digital readout cycled through a dozen different diagnostics.

An unfamiliar woman sat at a desk to my left, surrounded by an array of holoscreens and focused on her work. The person on my right was much more attentive.

"Rich?" Carl leaned forward in his chair and pressed his hand into my own. "Can you hear me?"

"Carl." My voice croaked as I spoke. "Good to see you, pal. Where am I? Cetie or Cetif? Hopefully the former."

"Ah...Cetie," said Carl, a hint of confusion marring his look of otherwise complete relief. "Pylon Alpha General Hospital to be specific. My goodness, Rich, am I glad to see you awake. How are you feeling?"

"Parched," I said. "Could I get a glass of water?"

"You bet. Flavia?"

The woman gave a thumbs up. "Signals look good. Go for it."

Carl sprang to action, filling a cup from a sink on the side of the room and bringing it over. I lifted an arm to accept it, but my muscles felt creaky and weak. Function they did, though, so I took the cup and drained it.

"Better," I said as I brought it down. I nodded at the woman. "Who's that?"

"Flavia Applestone," said Carl. "She's a tech expert with the PAPD. She's picked up some medical expertise over the past few days, too."

The woman waved idly at me without turning from her holoscreens.

"Got it," I said. "Carl? I think I have some idea of what you're going to tell me, but perhaps you could fill me in on a few things? Namely, what the heck happened and how did I get here?"

Carl nodded. "What's the last thing you remember?"

"The last thing I remember is shooting myself in the head, but I have a feeling that didn't actually happen. So why don't you tell me your side of the story."

Carl's eyes widened, and he blinked. "Um...right. I suppose I should've expected something like that. To make a long story short, it appears you've been in some sort of artificially induced Brain coma. I first became concerned when after ten hours logged onto the Princess Gaming servenets, you still hadn't disconnected."

"This is when I went in to interview Lars Busk's friends, right?" I said. "The ones who were playing Marked 4 Death?"

"That's right," said Carl.

"How long ago was that?" I asked.

"A little over a week."

A week? Wow. "Alright. Sorry to interrupt. Keep going."

"I gave you a little more time," said Carl, "but within short order you'd lost control of your bowels. I tried to get ahold of Paige to force you out of the simulation, but much to my surprise, I couldn't. Electronic communications to Paige went right through unanswered, just as our communication attempts to Lars had. The only difference of course is I'd assumed Lars had been ignoring our Brain missives. I knew Paige wouldn't do the same."

Not under normal circumstances, said Paige.

Hey, girl, I said. *It's good to hear your voice again. You've been mostly absent.*

That's an understatement, she said. *I wish I could tell you what happened, but the fact of the matter is I'm as lost as you are. I only recently managed to reboot. Last thing I recall is trying to exit the Princess simulation after speaking with TriumphCat. Hopefully Carl can fill us both in on the rest.*

"Well, after unsuccessful attempts to rouse the two of you, I thought to check the Princess Gaming servenets, and sure enough, you showed up as online and in game," said Carl. "That's when I knew something was afoot. First, I contacted Princess themselves, but their customer service representatives told me it must've been a glitch on our end, as their own internal records showed me as online but inactive. That's when I contacted the police.

"Luckily, Officer Sanz was more than happy to listen to my story, and he didn't dismiss it out of hand. He came over as soon as he was able with Officer Applestone in tow. So began a flurry of calls to various Gen-Born technical support lines during which Applestone attempted a number of maneuvers to try to force you from the simulation—or wherever it was you were. They all failed. Your Brain had totally shut down, taking you with it."

"I suspected a malicious attack," said Flavia, turning her head toward me, "but of which kind, I wasn't sure. I'd never seen anything like it. We detected wireless activity originating within your Brain, but we couldn't track it, and none of the more fundamental elements of your Brain architecture responded to external probe. It was kind of cool in a mysterious, unnerving sort of way. Glad to see you're okay, by the way."

"Thanks," I said. "So what happened then?"

"Soon after, it became apparent you'd need medical attention," said Carl, "so we brought you here to Pylon Alpha General and started to monitor you. We tried a number of different strategies, but none of them worked—until now."

I took a deep breath. "Wow. I suspected as much. Eventually, anyway."

Carl tapped his head. "So...what exactly went on up there? If Paige was as incapacitated as she claims, you're the only one with knowledge of your mind's events."

"You want the long version, or the short version?"

"The long, eventually," said Carl. "I'll settle for the short first."

"I came out of the simulation," I said. "Or at least I thought I did. But not long after I'd exited, a guy by the name of Dirk Kriggler dropped by and—well, I said I'd stick to the short version, so let's just say he led me on a long, strange, unbelievable quest. Eventually, the sheer number of improbable events I encountered led me to realize what I thought was reality couldn't be. That's when it dawned on me that I must still be in the simulation."

Carl smiled and glanced at Flavia. "It sounds like our plan worked then."

"Your *plan?*" I said. "What are you talking about? I told you, I figured it out. I forced the simulation's hand to kick me out."

"You undoubtedly did," said Flavia, turning toward me in her chair, "but you had help. After our initial failures, we sat down and came up with a new plan of attack. Based off the details of the Busk case, Officer Sanz and your friend Carl came up with a theory that closely mirrored what you just described. I'd already suspected your Brain was the subject of a malicious attack, and since it had occurred while you were in the Princess simulation, it made sense the sim might be keeping your conscious mind prisoner. While I couldn't restore your Brain through normal channels, I did find a backdoor, possibly the same one through which the attack occurred, that let me inject my own code. I won't go into the technical details, but basically, I delivered an inversely correlated adaptive probabilistic servenet hacking function into your Brain and hoped for the best."

"Say what now?" I said.

"Officer Applestone fought fire with fire," said Carl, "attacking the malicious code with more code that would function to make the improbable probable."

"Like you shooting a man?"

Carl's eyes widened. *"I shot someone?"*

"In the reality I experienced, yes," I said. "But I'd like to think I would've ferreted out the truth of the matter on my own sooner or later. Kriggler was too much of a caricature, as if he'd been pulled from one of the old private detective vid docs I'm so fond of, and my skill with a firearm was unheard of. It reminded me of playing Marked 4 Death on the easiest setting all over again. Speaking of which, we should check on Lars's friends and his girlfriend, TriumphCat. If I was targeted with a malicious hack, there's a good chance they were, too. I spoke to them about Lars's disappearance, and I shared my suspicions."

"So you think this is all related to Lars's death?" said Carl.

"I don't see how it wouldn't be," I said. "Lars dies while hooked into a Princess Gaming servenet that registers him as online even after death, and then I suffer the same fate—all except for the death part. It has to be connected."

"You remember the names of the avatars you talked to?" asked Flavia.

Paige reminded me, and I passed them along.

"Thanks," said Flavia, standing up. "I'll have teams check into these. In the meantime, I've notified Officer Sanz you're awake. He should be here soon. I suspect he'll have a slew of questions for you."

"I wouldn't expect it any other way," I said.

Flavia nodded and exited the room. Carl stayed in place, continuing to shower me with his warm smile.

"Have you been here the whole time?" I asked.

"Where else would I go?"

His smile infected me. "Thanks, pal. I appreciate it."

"Of course," he said. "I'd do anything for you. You know...except kill a man."

"Yeah, I'm happy to leave that one behind me in the simulation," I said. "But now that the officer's gone, be straight with me. What's the status of Lars's investigation? I'm assuming it's being treated as a murder?"

"To my knowledge, yes," said Carl, "but I'm not being kept in the loop. You'll have to ask Officer Sanz, and I'm not sure how forthcoming he'll be with answers."

"Questions, yes. Answers, probably not. Although, he might be more forthcoming if I apologize and give him a full statement. I did that in the simulation, but I guess I haven't done it in real life yet." I sighed and leaned back into the cushions behind me. For hospital issue, they weren't too bad.

"Rich?"

I glanced at Carl. "Yes?"

"I know you've been locked in your own reality and that environment may not have been conducive to thoughts of the events here in the real world, but during the times I haven't spent worrying, I can't help but wonder *why* someone would murder Lars. He didn't have anything of value to take. Any power to speak of. Any relationship squabbles, unless there was one with his online girlfriend. So if he was murdered—why?

And why go to such great lengths, including making an attempt on your life, to cover it up?"

I shook my head. "I don't know, Carl. I actually *did* think about that in my simulated reality. Dirk Kriggler, the PI, initially came to my apartment because he'd been investigating a similar case. That's how he managed to convince me to tag along with him. Honestly, I wouldn't have followed him if not for the similarities between his case and Busk's. In fact..."

Carl waited a moment for my response. "In fact, what?"

I blinked. I'd heard of life imitating art, but what if in this case, it was the other way around?

"Carl?" I said. "Has anyone bothered to check into Lars's finances?"

28

I sat in the back of a police cruiser, gliding along a remote road located somewhere between thirteen and fourteen hundred kilometers south of Pylon Alpha, near the Cetie equator. Leafy palm fronds shadowed our car while thick walls of underbrush rose up on either side of us, threatening to overtake the road if the traffic lessened for even a day. While the self-healing pavement resisted the effects of the sun, rain, and heat remarkably well, there was only so much it could do against the relentless assault of biology.

Our car jostled as we travelled over an overzealous root that saw the road as a new, hostile territory to be conquered. Ahead of us, the tall SWAT van which we followed rammed into a low hanging tree branch, sending it swaying and bouncing. I startled as a half-dozen bangs sounded out, all while orangish yellow fruits bounced off the roof of our car into the surrounding jungle.

I glanced behind us as we sped past. "Did we just get...*mangoed?*"

Carl, who sat across from me, seemed thoroughly nonplussed. "One of the many dangers of living in the tropics, I suppose, up there with disease and enormous bugs."

Officer Sanz, who rode next to me in the car, was similarly unimpressed. He continued to gaze out the window silently, as he'd done for the past half hour.

"Sanz?" I said.

He turned. "Yes?"

"I don't think I've had a chance to thank you for letting me tag along on this excursion."

The officer cracked a smile. "Oh, you've had a chance. Several."

I snorted. I'd become so used to his official guise, I'd failed to realize the guy might actually have a personality. "Let me rephrase that. Thanks for letting me tag along."

"Not a problem," he said. "To be fair, we probably wouldn't have broken this case without your help."

"Really?" I said. "You mean that?"

"Absolutely," said Sanz. "If you hadn't been attacked by a malicious piece of code, we probably never would've classified Busk's death as a homicide, and without that we wouldn't be where we are now."

"Oh," I said. "I thought you were going to praise me for suggesting you look into Busk's finances. Because without *that,* we wouldn't be here."

Sanz shook his head. "No, actually. As soon as we opened a murder investigation into Busk's death, we looked into his finances by default. It was simply a mat-

ter of time until we sifted through the data and realized..." Sanz stared at me and his face softened. "I
mean...sure. Thanks for the suggestion. It really put us
on the right path."

"You're a terrible liar," I said.

"Not as bad as you."

We took a turn around another patch of overgrown
shrubbery, and Sanz took a Brain call.

"Sanz here. Affirmative. Yes, I understand. Copy
that."

He signed off and elbowed me in the ribs. "The
SWAT leader says we're almost there. Do you remember the conditions we agreed to when we allowed you
to come?"

"Yes."

Sanz lifted an eyebrow. "I was allowing you a con-
venient opportunity to recite said conditions. You know,
for confirmation purposes."

"Oh. Given our previous banter, I thought we were
taking each other literally." I smiled. "But, since you
asked...it's simple. Carl and I stay in the car while you
and the SWAT team enter the compound. Once you
give me the all clear, we can come out."

Sanz nodded. "Good. Stick to that."

"Really, though," I said. "If the intelligence we've
gathered on this guy is accurate, you don't need to be
worried about my safety."

"One, you're putting too much faith in intelligence.
Two, you think I'm worried about your safety?" Sanz
snorted. "I want to make sure you don't get in the way."

I smiled again. "You're still a terrible liar."

"Get over yourself." He nodded toward the front. "Here we go. Stick to the plan."

Our car passed through a stone gate largely covered with ivy and transitioned onto a brick roadway. The chaotic jungle fell back, replaced instead with an environment just as green but several orders of magnitude better manicured. Palms stood isolated from one another, interspersed with ferns, philodendrons with large, triangular leaves, and bright green grass. Soon they gave way to a large circular driveway with an extravagant fountain at the center, and beyond that, a fantastic tropical mansion painted in white and cream featuring tall columns and a wraparound patio.

The SWAT van stopped at the front steps. Its back doors flung open, and a dozen armored police officers poured out. Our car came to a stop behind them, and Sanz darted out to join them.

The door to our cruiser closed automatically as Sanz and the special tactics officers rushed forward. They broke open the front doors with a swift blow from a portable battering ram and rushed into the gap, shouting orders with their pulse pistols drawn. Within seconds, they'd disappeared inside. The sounds of their entrance faded, and I was left staring at the front door.

Seconds passed, turning into a minute. I glanced at Carl. "So, uh...what's new with you?"

"Not much," he said. "Except while you were in a coma, I finally went ahead and got that compact fusion upgrade to my power generation systems."

"*What?*" I said. "No way. You know I expressly forbade that."

"Relax," said Carl. "I'm kidding. The Carl from your simulation didn't do much of that, did he? It's how you know you're not still in a virtual reality."

"Don't even joke about that," I said. "You know that's going to give me nightmares for the rest of my life."

Sanz's voice crackled in my mind. *We got him, Rich. You're free to come out.*

I gave Carl a nod. We exited the cruiser, headed up the stairs, and entered the mansion. An opulent foyer stretched out before us, with twin staircases winding up the sides heading into a central room on the second floor. A pair of SWAT officers were in the process of dragging a man through the double doors at the top, a man with unruly bronze hair, a similar reddish brown beard, and wearing a set of purple silk pajamas. He sported a look of confusion on his face as he struggled weakly against the officers' grip, all the while mumbling incoherently about his innocence and rights and the general outrage of his arrest.

I knew precisely who he was. Vicente Caetano, former Princess Gaming CEO and co-founder. With Officer Sanz at our side, or rather vice versa, we'd performed quite the investigation into him after finding out that, similar to the simulation in which I'd been trapped, the majority of the money from Lars Busk's accounts had been removed following his death. The process of tracking down the funds had been nontrivial, but between the efforts of Flavia, a few other police technical wizards, and the banks they delivered compliance orders to, they'd eventually tracked the funds to none other than Caetano.

At first, it hadn't made much sense, at least until we started delving into the history of Caetano and the company he'd founded. Although the man was a brilliant programmer and gaming visionary, which helped him build a rabid customer base at Princess, he'd struggled with some of the more monetarily-oriented aspects of running a successful business, namely marketing and sales. In part because of that and in part because of his reputedly abrasive personality, Caetano had eventually seen his company turn against him. In a secret meeting, the board of directors led by then member Johnny Masters had bought Caetano out of his shares of the company in a hostile takeover, subsequently promoting Masters to the spot of president and CEO. The animosity didn't end there, however, as the company then went through a series of legal gymnastics to not only ensure Caetano would never again have a say in Princess's affairs, but they even stripped the man of his pension, benefits, and—gasp—deleted his avatar.

Of course, Caetano's fortune was large enough that the loss of his pension probably didn't inconvenience him, but that hadn't stopped him from taking out his furor on Princess's remaining customer base and recouping the losses where possible. As we'd found, Busk wasn't the only one being fleeced and affected by the same malicious Brain worm that had attacked me. Sanz and his fellow officers had thus far found dozens of others—some alive, some dead, and some still unaccounted for. All of them fit the same profile. Loners, Intros, and heavy gamers that wouldn't be missed—at least not at first. Caetano would infect them with the malicious code, plunging them into a separate simulation upon signing off and simultaneously replacing their avatars with mirror-image NPCs in the Princess servenets.

If not for Lars's estranged mother looking to reconnect, who knows how long it would've taken for the gambit to be uncovered. Instead of the dozens who'd already been targeted, the numbers could've climbed into the hundreds, even thousands. Though Caetano was clearly responsible, the public relations crisis for Princess Gaming would've been disastrous, likely insurmountable. No one would ever again trust the company, and users would actively fear for their lives in the simulation, thus ensuring Princess's downfall. While I wasn't in the business of tracking down murderers, Officer Sanz assured me large-scale corporate revenge was a suitable motive for this sort of thing.

Caetano kept mumbling and shouting as the SWAT officers escorted him down the stairs, though it was obvious from the creakiness in his voice that he didn't use it much. Certainly not around other people. "Let g—go of me, I say. You've g—got the wrong g—guy! I'd never g—go after g—gamers. I love g—gamers! I love everything about g—gaming!"

"But not Princess Gaming, am I right?" said the cop at his side. "Now shut up and keep moving. Don't you know you have a right to remain silent?"

The two officers dragged Caetano through the front door, ripping his yells from the interior of the home and restoring a sense of peace. With Carl tracking me closely, I mounted the stairs and followed them into the room from which the officers had extracted Vicente. Inside, I found not his bedroom or a study or holoflick theater but the most extravagant gaming room imaginable. In the middle on a high pedestal sat an enormous gaming chair, padded with simulation breathable leather, equipped with a bevy of controls for temperature regulation, muscle stimulation, fluid replenishment, and even a mysteriously creepy 'body fluid detox.' A quick shower station stood in a corner of the room next to an autodresser, and a pair of extendable conveyers held freshly baked sweets and pre-prepared meals, likely for quick delivery to the central chair. I noticed the gaming rig was missing the standard pink Princess logo, however.

I walked around to the front of the chair, running my hand across the faux leather. I sighed and shook my head. "Why would someone do this, Carl? I mean, it takes a special kind of sick, twisted bastard to infect people with a virus that starves them to death. But to do it to a dozen people? That we know of?"

"It could've been thirteen," said Carl.

I glanced at my partner. "I know I've said it before, but thanks. For saving me."

He smiled. "You're welcome, Rich. But let's focus on how many others we both saved together."

I heard a knock on the door. It was Sanz.

"Hey," I said. "Find anything incriminating? A secret underground torture chamber, or a stash of child pornography, or a collection of political literature?"

Sanz shook his head. "Nothing so far. We haven't found any staff, or droids for that matter. Just your typical household maintenance and lawn care dumbbots. Between this gaming rig and the rest of the place, it comes across as your standard Intro gamer megaman-sion."

"Those come standard, now?" I asked.

Sanz gave me a look. "I'll have a few guys stay behind and canvass the place thoroughly, but that could take days. Seeing as we've got Caetano, I'm heading back. Can I give you a lift? Cabs take a while to summon out here."

I sighed. "I guess."

Sanz lifted an eyebrow. "Something on your mind?"

"It's nothing," I said. "I was just expecting the raid to be a bit more...dramatic."

"Like a tense gunfight against an army of battle droids?"

"I told you that in confidence."

"We got our guy," said Sanz. "Nobody got hurt. That's a win in my data file."

"I know," I said. "And I'm with you. Trust me, I don't want any more casualties. So what happens now?"

"What do you mean?" said Sanz. "We got the guy. Now we go home—*if* you'll accept my ride."

I caught a hint of a suggestion at the end there. "I hear you. Lead the way."

29

I gazed out the windows of our pod, past the transparent walls of our elevated, evacuated tube and at the blur of foliage beneath us, a streaky mess of green intermixed with the occasional splotch of brown. It was amazing how a natural landscape could turn into a modern art rendition at twelve hundred kilometers per hour. Somehow I didn't think that was how the original masters had found their inspiration.

I turned my focus back inside as we barreled along at high speed, probably forty minutes away from Pylon Alpha. Toward the front of the pod, a holoadvert transitioned from commercial to commercial in twenty second increments. One of the ads promoted Pylon Alpha's upcoming E43 Conference, Cetie's largest annual entertainment and gaming-related professional gathering. Thousands usually attended, though not necessarily the gamers themselves—most were too introverted to be able to make the trip. The advert cycled through a number of companies that would be making an appearance: Takachi Corp, Omegasoft, Triangular Helix, Verve, and of course, Princess Gaming.

As I watched the advert, my mind wandered to one of the news vids I'd watched with Officer Sanz, one from two years ago, right after the ouster of Vicente Caetano from Princess and right before that year's E43. The reporter, a lovely if somewhat shy and mousy woman who was sure to appeal to the gaming masses, had gone into detail about Caetano's ejection from the company, including the hostile takeover by Masters and his cronies, but the story didn't end there. She'd spoken via Brain with several die-hard Princess gamers, most of whom lamented Caetano's loss, especially to a sleazeball of Masters' magnitude, and who predicted Princess would suffer as a result. Perhaps in the end user product they'd been right, but in terms of profits, they couldn't have been more wrong. Sleazebag or not, Masters managed to bring in more users than ever before and come up with new schemes to separate them from their SEUs. Business boomed, company stock skyrocketed, and Masters headlined numerous parties emphasizing the company's newfound success and creative direction.

I'm sure Caetano had been thrilled.

"Are you doing alright?" Carl sat next to me. He eyed me with a twinge of concern.

I gave him a nod. "I'm fine."

"Still thinking about Caetano?"

He knew me too well. I'd never be able to pull the wool over his eyes unless I laid hands on a live sheep and some pruning shears. "I guess I still don't understand why he did it. Kill those poor people, I mean."

"Didn't we already discuss this?" said Carl. "To get back at Princess Gaming for throwing him out on his proverbial behind. Not that his landing spot was particularly unpleasant. If you ever get tired of your apartment, we could consider relocating to the tropics."

"The money, though," I said. "That's one of many things that don't add up. Look, I get Caetano might've been angry. Furious, in all likelihood—but at *Princess,* not the gamers themselves. He built that company from the ground up. Programmed the initial hub worlds and many of the immersive games on which the company staked its reputation. According to the news docs I skimmed through, he stayed active in the programming even after the company hired several hundred dedicated programmers, as well as countless other employees. And look at his home. There weren't any visitors, no family, no droids even. The entire focus gravitated around a gaming chair. By all accounts, third-hand and first-hand, the man's an avid gamer. Cares about little else. So why would he go after Princess's *gamers?*"

"I take it you don't like the explanation we decided upon," said Carl. "That by picking off Princess gamers one by one, he'd be able to do lasting damage to the company before anyone noticed."

"No, I think the explanation fits," I said, "or at least it would if Caetano were an unbalanced sociopath. But nothing we've seen about him supports that notion. Again, he loves gamers. Is an avid one himself, and according to the news vids I watched, the majority of Princess gamers, or at least those who were aware of him and his role, were saddened when Masters and company forced him out.

"More importantly, while the motive for getting back at Princess Gaming is solid, there are any number of other ways he could've gone about it, methods that wouldn't have involved murdering people. Take the worm we assume he created. Caetano is an expert programmer. It would've been easy for him to create something like that, especially with his knowledge of Princess's inner workings and servenet architecture. But I'll bet that for the code to work, it has to have infected Princess's servenets as well, otherwise how else would it be delivered to the end user? And if Caetano can hack into Princess's servenets, then there are any number of other ways he could've sabotaged the company. He probably could've taken the whole Princess grid offline, wiped the servenets, or something equally traumatic.

"And I'll tell you what else doesn't make sense. The money. Why would he take gamers' funds? He certainly didn't need them, given his success. He could've just as easily embezzled money from Princess's own coffers if I'm right about his hacking ability. And the biggest head-scratcher? In the malicious simulation that kept me prisoner, we tracked our killer through the dead gamers' bank accounts. Why would Caetano give me the clue to discovering his nefarious plot through his own simulation? It doesn't make any sense."

"Perhaps his malicious program was forced to adapt on the fly," said Carl. "As far as we know, all of the people Caetano targeted were loners. He probably didn't expect to have one of his mark's relatives come looking for them. When you came poking and prodding, the code that attacked you, which until then probably had only been used to make the victims think they were in their apartments and continuing to play Princess games, had to change. Surely Caetano himself wasn't directing all the minutia you experienced, so the program did what it could. That could explain why it created Kriggler as it did, based off old private eye vid docs, or why it used a version of Caetano's own scheme as the basis for the plot of your simulated experience."

"It's possible," I said. "But I think someone smart enough to create a program of such destructive potential in the first place would've put a few more preventative measures in place. And let's not forget that beyond infecting people, his malicious code also successfully impersonated those same people in the Princess simulation, otherwise TriumphCat and the rest of Lars's friends would've noted his absence. Whatever it is, that code is inside the Princess servenets."

"Then we should warn them when we return," said Carl. "If there's lingering malicious code in their servenets, they'll want to know."

"Yes," I said. "We *should* warn them."

I sat back in my chair, chewing on my thoughts. The problem with my suppositions, of course, was that if Caetano wasn't the culprit, then who was? Even if it didn't make total sense for him to have executed the evil plot, all the evidence pointed to him, and he had a solid motive for action. Would anyone have a reason to set him up?

A clock at the front of the pod ticked forward methodically while the adverts continued to run.

Paige? I said.

Yes, my prince?

Can you load up that keynote address from last year's E43 conference? I asked. *The one from Princess Gaming?*

Sure thing.

My vision faded, and I was transported inside the Pylon Alpha Civic Coliseum. A crowd of thousands cheered as Johnny Masters took the stage, and he responded with one of his used spaceship salesman smiles. He thanked them, and once the cheers subsided, he launched into a prepared speech, talking through bullet points about Princess's wonderful upcoming game lineup, their commitment to the gamer, and their innovative team of programmers and content creators.

"Trust me folks," he said. "This year is going to be Princess Gaming's *best* in terms of game quality and immersion. Our sims will be the most lifelike, the most exciting, and the most engrossing of any provider's, on this or any other planet. And you know why we do it? Because at Princess Gaming, we don't just serve the customer. We *are* the customer. We love to game as much as every single one of you. That's why our quality is second to none. Because at Princess Gaming, *we get gamers!*"

As the crowd cheered and Masters soaked it up, I thought back to my initial encounter with Masters' avatar in the Princess Gaming new user orientation. He'd claimed he'd been built to be an *exact replica* of the real Masters, indistinguishable in every way, an NPC but a perfect copy of the real thing. In addition to making numerous claims about getting gamers, he'd also confessed to being a lifelong Intro, just like his gaming vassals.

And yet there he stood, in front of a roaring crowd of thousands, smiling and loving every second of it.

30

I stood in a darkened corridor at the Pylon Alpha Civic Coliseum, in one of the maintenance areas directly behind the main stage. Heavy cables for moving equipment stretched across the rafters above me, as did power cords for lights and audio equipment and holo-projectors. Through the barrier at my side, I could hear the muffled roar of the assembled crowd, as well as the equally muffled blare of the presenter's voice through the coliseum's speakers.

Officer Sanz gave me a nudge. "Sounds like it's about over. You ready?"

"I'm ready," I said. "Once again, thanks for letting me and Carl tag along."

Carl gave Sanz a tip of his head at the mention.

"No problem," said Sanz. "You earned it. Same plan as last time then. Stay out of the way and let me do the talking."

"Not exactly the same plan, then," I said. "Otherwise Carl and I would still be in the cruiser."

"And I can still send you back there," said Sanz. "Don't make me regret this."

I pulled my fingers across my lips, indicating their sealed-ness.

Sanz tilted his head, listening to the speech. At a particular cue, he waved his hand. "That's it. Let's go."

We snaked our way through the back of the space, past control boards and display interfaces, until we reached the edge of the stage at the front. There, we joined forces with a pair of police officers and a member of the coliseum security. From our vantage point out of view at stage right, I could hear the cheers of the crowd and see the man they showered with applause: Princess CEO and president, Johnny Masters. If not for the color of his suit being different, the scene looked identical to the holovid I'd watched of the E43 conference from a year ago.

Masters pressed his hands together as the crowd continued to cheer, then waved and headed off the stage in our direction.

The security guard hailed him at the edge of the curtains. "Excuse me. Mr. Masters? Some men here to see you."

Masters tried to brush past us. "Yes. Johnny Masters, nice to meet you. Look, I'm extremely busy with the festivities, so I'll need you to contact my secretary. She should be able to—"

Sanz snagged him before he could weasel away. "Johnny Masters? You're under arrest for the murder of twelve men and women, the attempted murder of twenty more, with charges still pending on a half-dozen others. You have the right to remain silent, and anything you say can and will be used against you in the court of law. You have the right to counsel with an attorney, and—"

"Whoa, whoa, whoa," said Masters as Sanz cuffed his hands behind his back. *"Arrested?* For the murder of twelve people? *Are you insane?* What the hell is wrong with you? Don't you know who I am? You're dealing with Johnny Masters here, damn it!"

"You can drop the act, Masters," said Sanz. "We accessed the Princess Gaming servenets by subpoena. We found the traces of the malicious code you installed there, same as the code we found in the victims of your cyber attacks, and we tracked it through your company's internal systems back to a dummy account. To be fair, it was smart of you not to upload the code into the servenets from your own master account. What wasn't smart was providing the dummy account with a security access level only you and Princess's chief security officer could've authorized, or waiting until your CSO was off site to give your dummy account said access so the CSO wouldn't notice. We also found the code funneling you data from the feedback sensors in the specialty Mark VI Princess Gaming rigs each of your victims happened to possess, providing you with information about their gaming, eating, and sleeping habits, as well as giving you a spy channel into their apartments to convince you they were good targets. So trust me, it's in your best interests to shut up and come along peacefully."

Sanz didn't give Masters much of a choice in the latter. He grabbed him firmly by the arm and pulled him toward the doors, with the two police officers flanking him on either side. Carl and I brought up the rear, completing the phalanx and preparing ourselves for combat—not that it would be necessary. The conference goers on the main exhibit floor parted in front of us like a sea, none of them the least bit interested in getting in our way, though most of them muttered and pointed and gossiped and undoubtedly filmed our excursion for posting on the public servenets.

Masters kept up his protests as he walked, though his ferocity and vigor ebbed ever so slightly. "You have no idea who you're dealing with. I'm Johnny fricking Masters, the most powerful man in gaming! I'll have a swarm of lawyers so thick and so talented buzzing around me that you won't even know when I'll be acquitted. You'll find out third-hand, from a courier who delivers the message to the cardboard box where you'll be living after my guys get through with you. This isn't over. Not by a long shot!"

We exited through the front doors, into the Cetie heat, and kept walking. Down the steps, to the trees that lined the side of the road, and over to the police cruiser Sanz had parked there. As we approached, Sanz activated the car doors, which popped open for Masters' admission.

I'd kept my mouth shut the entire time, but I couldn't leave without some form of justification from Masters, some parting shot fired from the muzzle of my own pistol. Not after what I'd gone through at the hands of his malicious simulation.

"Why'd you do it, Masters?" I asked as we stopped outside the car. "Why'd you kill all those people? What was it? Some sick game to you? Payback to Caetano? If so, for what?"

Masters eyed me, as if noticing me for the first time. "Who the hell are you?"

"Rich Weed, private investigator," I said. "I'm the one who found one of your targets, Lars Busk, dead, and I'm the one you tried to take out when I came probing in the wake of Busk's death. You could say I'm the reason you're headed behind bars."

It could've been my imagination, but it seemed as if Masters' face hardened as I spoke. His eyes grew more steely, and his jaw tightened—a surprising response for a man as innocent as he proclaimed to be.

He spoke in a tight voice. "What? You think I'm going to stand here and confess? To what? Some heinous crime? You're even stupider than you look."

"Not as stupid as you," I said. "I'm not the one who programmed his online avatar to act *exactly* like him, including being as big a liar as he is. To claim you're a gamer, an Intro, when all evidence points to the contrary. Did you really think that would fly? How dumb do you think gamers are?"

I didn't think it would be possible, but Masters' face hardened even more, and a pall fell over it. When he spoke, he did so slowly, menacingly, and from a place of intense loathing.

"Why do you care?" he said. "I can tell you're not one of them. An *Intro*. A *gamer*, like that insufferable prick Caetano. You think their lives are worthwhile? Something to be cherished, to be lauded? *No.* They sit all day in their chairs, oblivious to the reality around them, wasting food, wasting resources, wasting the very air we breathe while those few of us who remain, the doers, the thinkers, the Extros, *we* are the one who craft the worlds, the real ones and the fakes. Is that even really living? When your entire existence can be boiled down to a series of repetitive actions, a life spent inside a representation of reality, and when your entire conscious being can be replaced by a carefully pro-grammed piece of code, a non-player character? These people you claim were targeted by some madman? You say their lives were snuffed out, but it sounds as if not much has changed. Are you sure they weren't merely lines of code on a servenet?"

I narrowed an eye and glanced at Sanz. "Did he just say what I think he said?"

"Not really," said Sanz. "He's too smart to have ad-mitted to anything. Now shut up and get in the car."

Again, Officer Sanz didn't give him much choice. He put one hand on Masters' shoulder and another on his head and pushed him into the vehicle. The two officers who'd accompanied us followed him in. Sanz hung back and closed the doors. The sound of the cruiser's electric motor whirred into action, followed promptly by the whine of the air conditioner restoring the cab's interior temperature.

"*Insufferable prick Caetano,*" I said as Sanz turned back to me. "I wonder what he did to earn Masters' ire?"

"Must've slighted him at some point," said the offi-cer. "Clearly Masters hates gamers but holds a special place in his heart for the ex-CEO. It would explain why he tried to frame the guy as well as take out as many Intro gamers as possible. We'll keep digging. We'll fig-ure it out."

"Speaking of Caetano," I said. "What's going to happen to him?"

"Oh, we'll let him walk," said Sanz. "And give him an apology for the way he was treated. Knowing his type, I'm sure he'll take it and run. Won't want any further confrontation."

"I wonder if, after the dust settles, Princess Gaming might welcome him back?" said Carl. "Masters was the instigator for his ousting, after all."

I shrugged. "Might not be a bad idea, if he's willing. They'll need to do something to weather the public relations nightmare they're staring in the face."

Silence stretched for a moment as we all retreated to our thoughts. The electric cruiser purred.

"Well...I should go." Sanz eyed me and gave me a nod. "Look, Rich, I know you're the one who keeps thanking me for being included in these arrests, but I feel I owe you some thanks as well. If not for your actions, both conscious and unconscious, I'm not sure we ever would've gotten to the bottom of this."

"Come on," I said. "You would've figured it out sooner or later."

"Probably," said Sanz. "Which is why I'm not about to award you a medal for your actions. But if nothing else, it would've taken us longer to do so, costing countless more lives. Believe it or not, you and Carl saved people. That's something to be proud of. Just promise me one thing, going forward."

"What's that?" I asked.

"Next time, when a police officer asks for your statement, be honest with them from the start. It'll save us a whole lot of trouble in the long run."

"I'll do it," I said. "*If* there's a next time."

Sanz snorted. "I like your optimism. Take it easy, friend."

He opened the cruiser doors and shuffled inside. As soon as he'd settled himself, the car doors closed back up, and with a light whirr, the vehicle sped off. I watched it fade into the heat glare radiating up off the pavement.

"So," said Carl. "What now?"

I turned to my lifelong pal. "What do you mean? We got Masters. I'm no police officer, but the evidence against him seems solid as a rock. I don't care how many lawyers he hires, I suspect he's going away for a long time. Life, probably. Depending on how old Masters is, that could be a long time indeed."

"That's not what I meant," said Carl. "When Officer Sanz told you to cooperate with police, you said you would—*if* there's a next time."

"You picked up on that, huh?"

"You expected it any other way?"

I stuck my hands in my pockets, took a deep breath, and let it out slowly. "I don't know, Carl. This case left a bad taste in my mouth. It's one thing to track down missing cats, or fend off a bunch of fundamentalist nutbags, or even track down a group of space pirates, but this? Dealing with a sick, twisted murderer who thinks people's lives are no more important than computer code? It's not something I want to deal with. Ever again."

Carl lifted an eyebrow. "Are you saying you want to hang up your hat and coat—metaphorically speaking, of course?"

"I don't know, Carl," I said. "If I'm not enjoying it, why keep at it? It's not as if I need the money. I didn't need it even before I received that windfall from the InterSTELLA case."

"But then what will you do to pass the time?" asked Carl. "The main reason you became a private eye was to challenge yourself and keep your mind fresh."

Oh, no, said Paige. *Here we go again. I'll fire up Smashblocks. Maybe with a few months more practice, you can beat your all time high score of twenty-one billion.*

I smiled. Given the severity of the case, Paige hadn't been quite as flippant as she'd normally been. It was good to have her back.

"No guys," I said. "I don't intend to sit around and play mindless Brain games all day. Trust me, after my time stuck in that malicious simulation, I don't have *any* desire to play those ever again."

So what then? said Paige. *You plan on settling down? Starting a family?*

I snorted. "Please."

"Well it sounds as if you have some sort of plan in mind," said Carl.

"Actually, I do," I said. "You know of all the things I took part in during that Brain simulation—the teamwork with that insufferable Kriggler, the delving into Cetif's seedy underbelly, the illogical droid battles—there was one itch I found that I enjoyed having scratched."

Chatting with a loquacious Tak arms dealer? offered Paige.

"No," I said. "Travelling the stars. With my own ship. I think I should buy the Kestrel Chinook Z-class after all."

Carl blinked and answered slowly. "That...wasn't what I expected to hear."

"You don't approve?"

"Not at all," he said. "I'm glad you made the sensible choice of going with the Chinook over a used freighter or some other nonsense."

"So you're with me, then?" I said. "You'll be my co-captain or first mate or chief officer or whatever the heck you want to call it?"

Carl clapped me on the shoulder. "I'd go to the ends of the universe with you, Rich. You know that."

So, said Paige. *Instead of Rich Weed, Private Eye, you'd be known as...what? Rich Weed, Interstellar Voyager?*

"I was thinking interstellar privateer, myself."

Privateer, said Paige. *That word doesn't mean what you think it means.*

"Fine, then," I said. "Rich Weed, interstellar voyager it is."

I smiled as the words rolled off my tongue. *Interstellar voyager.* As I spoke them out loud, I realized—you know what? I liked the sound of it.

ABOUT THE AUTHOR

Alex P. Berg is a mystery, fantasy, and science fiction author, a scientist, and a heavy metal aficionado. Connect with him at www.alexpberg.com. If you'd like to be notified when new books are released, please sign up for his mailing list on his website. You will only be contacted when new books come out, your address will never be shared, and you can unsubscribe at any time.

Word of mouth is critical to author success. If you enjoyed this novel, please consider leaving a positive review on Amazon. Even if it's only a line or two, it would be a *huge* help. Thanks!